For a Long Moment, Monica Stared at the Ghost.

"What—what do you want?" Monica finally asked, her voice little more than a whisper.

In answer, Allegra slowly reached her hand toward Monica. Then, she began to move toward Monica.

"No!" Monica shouted, turning away and beginning to run. Her heart was beating so hard it felt as if it would burst. She ran back through the stacks toward the front of the room. Stopping for breath, she noticed her whole body was trembling. Monica looked over her shoulder and gasped. The ghost-girl was right behind her, having effortlessly and gracefully followed along.

Again Allegra, wearing an imploring expression on her face, reached out her hand toward Monica.

She wants me, Monica thought. *But for what? To kill me?*

Books by Lynn Beach

Phantom Valley: The Evil One
Phantom Valley: The Dark
Phantom Valley: Scream of the Cat
Phantom Valley: Stranger in the Mirror
Phantom Valley: The Spell
Phantom Valley: Dead Man's Secret
Phantom Valley: In the Mummy's Tomb
Phantom Valley: The Headless Ghost
Phantom Valley: Curse of the Claw

Available from MINSTREL Books

Phantom Valley™

The Evil One

Lynn Beach

A MINSTREL® BOOK

PUBLISHED BY POCKET BOOKS

New York   London   Toronto   Sydney   Tokyo   Singapore

This book is a work of fiction. Names, characters, places and incidents are either the product of the author's imagination or are used fictitiously. Any resemblance to actual events or locales or persons, living or dead, is entirely coincidental.

A MINSTREL PAPERBACK *ORIGINAL*

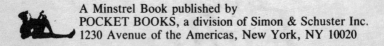

A Minstrel Book published by
POCKET BOOKS, a division of Simon & Schuster Inc.
1230 Avenue of the Americas, New York, NY 10020

Copyright © 1991 by Parachute Press, Inc.
Cover illustration copyright © 1991 by Lisa Falkenstern

ISBN: 0-671-74088-1

First Minstrel Books printing October 1991

10 9 8 7 6 5 4 3

PHANTOM VALLEY is a trademark of Parachute Press, Inc.

A MINSTREL BOOK and colophon are registered trademarks of Simon & Schuster Inc.

Printed in U.S.A.

To Holly and Monica

CHAPTER 1

I'M going to love it here! Monica Case thought, studying the building that would be her home for the next nine months. *It's going to be like living in the Old West.*

The school looked like a building from a western movie. She almost expected to see horse-drawn buckboards and women in long skirts sashaying by. Large and rambling, the dark wooden structure stood in front of a thick pine forest. From the roof of the front porch hung a black wooden sign with gold lettering: CHILLEEN ACADEMY.

Monica set her bag down on the lush lawn and pushed her long black hair out of her face. Staring at the building, she thought of the redbrick school she'd attended back home. She wondered what her friends would think if they could see her new school. She closed her eyes a moment and tried to imagine that it was one hundred fifty years earlier and that she was a pioneer just arriving in the West.

"Whoa! Watch out!"

Monica jumped at the cry and stepped out of the way to avoid being hit by a girl doing cartwheels across the lawn.

1

"I'm sorry!" said the girl, righting herself. "Are you all right?" She brushed a blond curl from her face and smiled sheepishly.

"I'm fine," said Monica, wondering if the girl was a little crazy.

"The grass looked so soft and cool, I decided to practice my floor routine," said the girl. "I'm on the gymnastics team."

"Really?" said Monica. "I'm planning to try out."

"Can you do back flips?"

"Sure," said Monica. "My best event is the balance beam." Holding her arms out to her sides, Monica ran through a couple of tricks in a routine she had practiced at least a hundred times.

"That was great," said the girl. "My name's Kim Harris, by the way."

"Monica Case."

Kim gave her a grin so wide that her eyes became slits, practically disappearing in her round face. She had short, very curly blond hair above a sprinkling of cinnamon-colored freckles. "Did you just get here?"

"Yeah," said Monica. "It was a last-minute thing. My dad's an architect, and a couple of weeks ago he got an assignment in Italy that'll last a few months. He's there now with my mom and baby sister."

"How come you didn't go?" said Kim.

Monica laughed. "I don't speak Italian. No, really, I didn't want to go to an Italian school. By the time I got used to it, it would be time to come home again. Besides, I've always wanted to live out West, and my aunt says Chilleen is a good school."

"It is," said Kim. "Especially for the kids who live here."

"Doesn't everyone?" Monica was surprised.

"Some of us are day students," said Kim. "Like me. I live in town with my parents."

"How long have you been going here?"

"This is my second year," said Kim. "I really like Chilleen, but it would be neater to actually stay here—even if it *is* spooky."

"Spooky?"

"There are all kinds of eerie stories about the academy," said Kim. "I'll tell you some of them later." She noticed Monica's small bag. "Is that all you brought?"

"We shipped the rest."

"Well, since you missed orientation, Monica, I'll show you around."

Inside the big dayroom, Chilleen Academy looked even more rustic and old with its polished wide wooden floorboards. Hung on every wall were framed paintings and photographs of Western scenes: high, pine-covered mountains, red-rocked canyons, sandy mesas, and plains. Even the furniture was rugged and solid. Tile-topped tables were surrounded by wood-and-cowhide chairs, and carved wooden benches lined the walls. The only thing that seemed out of place was a large-screen television set against one wall, with a handful of girls and boys in front of it.

"The whole academy used to belong to the Chilleen family," Kim explained, sweeping her hand around the dayroom. "That's where the name comes from."

"Who were the Chilleens?" said Monica.

"A pioneer family who helped settle the valley. They had terrible luck from the time they got here, and over the years all kinds of awful things happened to them."

"Like what?" said Monica. Stories about the past always interested her.

"Lots of things." Kim pulled Monica to a large window and pointed outside. "A Chilleen and his son once froze to death during a snowstorm there in the yard, thirty feet from the house. They didn't know how close they were."

"What bad luck!"

"Yeah," said Kim. "Supposedly all the ghosts of the Chilleens who died violently still walk around the academy."

"Cool," said Monica. "But does anyone actually believe that stuff?"

Kim gave her an odd look. "You'd be surprised. Lots of people believe it. Phantom Valley is a very strange place. For one thing, the animals around here somtimes act as if they're haunted. They roam around the burial grounds and Shadow Village, and are said to carry with them the spirits of the canyons. And people have heard all sorts of strange noises coming from the Chilleen family graveyard."

Monica raised an eyebrow. "Do you mean there's a graveyard right on the grounds?"

"It's out in the woods somewhere," said Kim. "I've never gone there—it's too scary for me." She stopped in front of a massive polished wood door. "This is Mrs. Danita's office. She's the headmistress. You've got to check in with her. I'll wait for you on the front porch, and when you're done I'll show you how to get to your room."

*   *   *

Monica left the headmistress's office with her mind and heart racing in excitement. She had filled out the necessary forms, but only half listened while Mrs. Danita explained about the required work-study jobs, which rotated every six weeks, and about "lights-out" and other school rules. Monica didn't care about any of that. All she could think about was getting settled in her new room, which, from Mrs. Danita's description, sounded wonderful.

The office and the other old-fashioned rooms she had peeked in were so much more spacious and airy than those of the boxy, white-walled apartment she shared with her parents and little sister. Also the bright, clear sky and spicy-smelling air were welcome changes from the noisy, smoky city where she lived. Strangely, even though she already missed her family, Monica felt oddly at home. *I belong here,* she thought.

She found Kim waiting on the front porch. The girl was standing bent over with her palms flat on the floor, apparently lost in thought. Kim straightened up as soon as she saw Monica.

"Where's your room?" Kim asked. "Let's see your key."

Monica handed it to her. "Mrs. Danita says I'm the first person to stay in this room."

"Really?" said Kim. She squinted at the number on the key and then whistled. "Whoa!" she said. "Maybe you ought to ask for another room."

"Why?"

Kim seemed embarrassed and then a little frightened. "Well," she said, "you're in the haunted wing."

Monica stared at Kim for a minute. "Haunted?" she said. "If that's true, I can't wait!" She followed Kim through the dayroom, toward the back of the house. "Is part of the academy really haunted?"

"Supposedly," said Kim, leading Monica into a hallway. "It's the oldest part of the house, but there are only a few dorm rooms there. They've been renovating some of it."

As they passed through a wide double door, Monica felt a chill, as if the temperature had suddenly dropped.

"It's cold in this part of the house, isn't it?" said Kim, grinning at her. "It's supposed to have something to do with the foundation being made out of a different kind of stone than the rest of the house."

Monica laughed. "If you're trying to scare me, it won't work. I think this is excellent."

"Well, good," said Kim after leading her up a long flight of polished wooden stairs. "Because here's your room."

"Mrs. Danita told me it once belonged to one of the last Chilleens to live here at the turn of the century," said Monica. "Her name was Allegra."

"Allegra Chilleen," said Kim slowly. "I've heard that name before. I wonder if she was one of the Chilleens who died in the fire."

"What fire?"

"There was a terrible fire in this wing back in the early nineteen hundreds. The entire place nearly burnt down, and the whole family died in the fire. It was such a disaster that even when the rest of the building was rebuilt, this wing stayed boarded up. When the school took over, new wings were added, but this wing was left alone. But about a year ago, they started running out of space and decided to renovate this wing and convert it into dorm rooms.

6

THE EVIL ONE

Some people say the Chilleens who died in the fire are still here. . . . At least that's one of the stories that's been passed around. But," Kim added with a grin, "as I told you, there are a lot of stories about the Chilleens."

"I want to hear all the stories!" said Monica.

"I don't know them all." Kim glanced at her watch. "And I've got to get home and help my mom with dinner. Well, have a good time unpacking, and I'll see you tomorrow."

"See you tomorrow," Monica echoed. She watched Kim bound down the stairs, taking them two at a time; then Monica opened the door to her room.

CHAPTER 2

FROM the second she saw the small, cheery room painted a sunny pale yellow, Monica fell in love with it. The ceiling was low and sloped from the center toward two opposite walls. Along one low wall was a window, and on the other was a small closet with a door only as high as Monica's chest. The woodwork was natural wood varnished to a high gloss.

Monica tried to imagine what the room had been like when Allegra lived there. Except for electricity, lamps, and light bulbs, the room didn't look as if it had been changed much since the early 1900s. The renovation had been carefully done to retain the right period and time.

Allegra would have had candles or a kerosene lamp. She'd probably have had a porcelain washbasin and pitcher on a stand, and wrapped, heated bricks would have warmed her bed on cold nights. Also the room wouldn't have smelled of fresh paint as it did now.

Monica opened the window and peered out at the clear sky above the dark pine forest. She imagined herself practicing back flips down on the thick lawn—something she'd never been able to do in the city. *It's perfect*, she thought. *Everything here is perfect.*

Monica felt more than a little shy when she entered the noisy dining hall an hour later. *If only Kim were here*, she thought.

She put a plate of macaroni and cheese and a green salad on her tray and checked around for a place to sit. At a table directly across the room, half a dozen girls and boys were talking and laughing louder than anyone else in the hall. One of the girls, a very pretty brunette with short, glossy hair, was the obvious center of attention. Monica watched as several other students waved and called out to the dark-haired girl.

I don't know a single person here, Monica thought in sudden despair. *How am I ever going to make friends?* She took her tray to a half-empty table and sat down to poke at her macaroni.

"Hi, there."

Monica raised her head and was startled to see a short, chubby boy with red hair standing across the table from her.

"My name's Jimmy Toliver," he said. "I'm new here."

"Me, too," said Monica, suddenly feeling more relaxed. "I'm Monica Case."

Jimmy sat down with a friendly smile. "I'm from California. How about you?"

"I'm from back East," she said. "Philadelphia. This is my first time in the West."

"Most of the West isn't like Phantom Valley," said Jimmy. "At least not the part I'm from. Most of it's modern like the rest of the country, with cities and freeways—not empty spaces and forests."

"That's what I like about it here," said Monica. "It's *not* modern, and I love the wide-open spaces. It seems as if you can see for miles."

They began to talk about the clean air when two girls, twins named Stacy and Tracy, asked to join them. They told Monica and Jimmy about life in Phantom Valley—about hiking and horseback riding, the farm animals they cared for, and their teachers and classes. By the time she'd finished eating, Monica felt as if she'd gone to Chilleen for years.

Monica and her new friends went into the dayroom to continue talking. Finally she made herself break away and said good night. She ran up the stairs to her room. The kids Monica had met at dinner lived in the other dorm wing and had roommates. Monica felt lucky to have a room to herself. It sure beat sharing a tiny cubbyhole with her baby sister as she did back home. This room was hers alone. Hers and Allegra's. At that thought she felt a slight shiver.

Don't go scaring yourself with made-up ghost stories, she told herself.

Suddenly exhausted from the long day, Monica crawled into bed. The light from the full moon poured in through the open window, making the room shimmer with a silvery glow. Outside, a lonesome howl sounded in the distance.

A coyote, Monica thought, drifting off to sleep and dreams of covered wagons and cool pine forests.

Crackle.

At the sudden noise, Monica opened her eyes. She'd

been dreaming, but couldn't remember what about. The digital clock beside her bed showed 3:00 A.M. Monica punched up her pillow and turned over. After a moment she felt sleep returning.

Crackle. Thump.

It's just the house settling, she thought.

Crackle.

Or maybe a branch is blowing against the roof.

Thump.

She opened her eyes, now completely awake. Outside the window, she could see treetops illuminated in the bright moonlight. They were still. Not a breath of wind was blowing.

Crackle. Thump. Thump.

Monica's heart began to beat faster. She sat up and listened carefully. The sounds seemed to be coming from the small closet.

Maybe it's an animal, she thought. *A mouse or a squirrel could have gotten trapped in there.*

She stepped into her slippers and padded across the floor to the small closet door. Cautiously she swung it open, half expecting to see a small animal come skittering out.

"Come on, little mouse," Monica said softly. "Or whatever you are. Come on out. I won't hurt you."

Silence. The noises had stopped.

Monica became aware then of a soft red light shining from the back of the closet. Perplexed, she ducked down and stepped inside. Now she could see that the light was shining in through a narrow crack at the back of the closet. It was coming from *behind* the closet. What could it be?

Curious, she reached back and felt around the crack. But all she could feel was the rough plaster wall. In spite of herself, Monica yawned. Whatever it was, she'd have to wait to check it out in the morning.

She closed the closet door and scooted back to bed. She had almost fallen asleep again when the bumping and crackling started over.

I'll worry about it tomorrow, she told herself, forcing her eyes closed. But the noises continued, fainter now but just as persistent. Glancing at the closet again, she saw a faint red glow outlining the entire door. It was as if something were trapped inside, desperately trying to get out.

CHAPTER 3

DESPITE being awake much of the night, Monica awoke early the next morning. She opened her eyes and glanced at the clock. It was only 6:00 A.M. Breakfast wouldn't start for another hour. She stayed in bed and let her eyes wander around the sunlit room, taking in every detail. Out her window she could see a brilliant sky and could hear the wake-up calls of the birds. It was a perfect day to begin classes in her new school.

Then she remembered the red glow from her closet and the strange noises she had heard the night before. *Maybe*, she thought, *I only imagined them.*

There was only one way to find out. She padded over to the small closet and pulled the door open. Pushing her clothes aside, she ducked low and moved toward the back of the closet. Sure enough, she found herself in front of a narrow crack on the back wall. Kneeling in front of it, she studied it closer and noticed that the crack was perfectly straight—probably man-made—and that it wasn't one but four cracks that outlined an area about the size of a medicine chest. In fact, the cracks seemed to form a door. *How exciting,* she thought. *Maybe it* is *a door.* She'd read enough mysteries to know that old houses sometimes had secret compartments. She pushed and pried at the cracks, but nothing budged. The door, if it was one, seemed to be painted shut. The painters probably hadn't even noticed it.

Monica backed out of the closet and looked around for a fingernail file. When she found it, she went back into the closet and inserted it into part of the crack. It fit perfectly. Bits of new paint chipped off as she ran the file all along the square outlined by the crack. Now with the crack free, it was even more obvious that this was a door. Monica pushed her hands against the door, and suddenly, with a hoarse creak, it swung slowly open.

Monica scooted back, half expecting a trapped squirrel or mouse to jump out at her. But nothing moved in the dark cubbyhole. Cautiously she inched forward again and peered into the small compartment. Cobwebs hung along the edges, and a thick layer of dust lay on the floor. It looked as if no one had opened the door in years.

Bringing her face even closer, she narrowed her eyes to study the darkness. At first the small space appeared to be empty, but then she saw something wedged into the back. Something light, limp, and unmoving. Something with a tiny, round face—the face of a girl.

"It's a doll!" she cried with delight. Excited, Monica reached into the cubbyhole and pulled out the doll. Before closing the little door, she felt around and searched the compartment for anything else, but there was nothing but dust.

Back in her room, Monica gently brushed cobwebs and dust from the doll as she examined it closely.

The doll had a soft cloth body and a round white china face, delicately painted with rosy cheeks and lips. Long black eyelashes extended out over wide blue eyes, and the doll's long, taffy-colored hair fell in corkscrew curls over a ruffled pink dress.

Around its neck the doll wore a gold-colored chain strung with letters that spelled "All Your Wishes."

"This doll must be at least a hundred years old," Monica said out loud. She knew she should tell Mrs. Danita about it—but then decided not to. After all, *she* had found it in *her* room. The antique bed and chair belonged to the room, and so must the doll.

Monica couldn't take her eyes off the doll's beautiful face. She laid it on its back and watched the eyes close. Then she watched them open again as she sat the doll back up. The blue eyes seemed to stare at her.

The sudden sound of a bell made her jump. Knowing she had to hurry, she put the doll on top of her bureau, dressed quickly, and ran down to the dining hall. Most of the kids were already eating.

Monica grabbed a glass of orange juice and a bowl of oatmeal. She noticed Jimmy sitting alone and went to join him.

"Let's see your class list," Jimmy said, finishing up an egg-yolk-soaked piece of toast.

Monica handed him her schedule, which was printed on blue paper, and began to eat.

"English, math, history," Jimmy read aloud. "Sounds like a tough morning schedule. I've got all my hard classes in the afternoon."

"I like to get the hard stuff over with first," said Monica. "Then I can relax in the afternoon, with art, Spanish—and gymnastics, my favorite."

"I hear the teachers are really tough here," he went on. "My roommate told me they give lots of homework."

"I don't mind," said Monica. "I just love it here."

But by her third-period history class, Monica was beginning to wonder if Jimmy had been right. Even though it was only the first day, the teachers were already loading on the homework. How would she be able to keep up with it all? It seemed as if Chilleen was going to be a lot harder than her old public school.

After art, she dropped her books off in her room and pulled out her gym bag. Gymnastics, she thought, would be different from her other classes. After all, she'd been the best gymnast at her old school. She worked hard at it, but not because she had to: gymnastics came easily to her.

Then she had an unsettling thought. Maybe she wouldn't be the star here. Maybe she wouldn't even make the team. After all, Chilleen was much tougher academically; maybe the competition in sports would be just as tough.

By the time she got to the gym, Monica was more nervous than she'd been since the first time she tried the uneven parallel bars. It was only when she saw Kim, grinning and waving to her from across the gym, that she cheered up. Monica crossed the gym and sat beside her on the bleachers.

"Good afternoon, girls," said a short woman with curly brown hair. "I'm Ms. Potter, and I'll be coaching gymnastics."

Several of the girls cheered.

"I'll start out testing you on the basics," Ms. Potter went on. "I want to see what each of you can do."

Monica felt comfortable as she demonstrated her leaps, midair splits, and tumbling finishes. She knew she did well. Her flips were straight and head-on, with perfect landings.

"Very good, Monica," Ms. Potter said from where she sat. "Now, let's see your vault off the horse."

"Sure," said Monica, wondering if she could do a vault as well as the other Chilleen students. The horse was the one piece of equipment she'd never quite gotten down. She took a deep breath, raised her hands, and stared at the horse. Finally lowering her arms, she ran for the beat board and pushed off—and fell off the horse, sprawling not too gracefully on the mat.

"Nice try," said Ms. Potter crisply. "You have a good takeoff, but we'll have to work on your dismount. Bridget Morgan? You're next."

Feeling embarrassed, Monica picked herself up and rejoined Kim. Before Monica could complain about her vault, Kim said, "Watch this," pointing to the center of the gym. When she saw where Kim was pointing, Monica recognized the popular dark-haired girl who'd been in the cafeteria the night before.

"Who is she?" Monica whispered.

"Her name's Bridget Morgan," said Kim. "I just call her 'Mor,' because she's got more of everything."

"What do you mean?"

"More money, more friends, more talent, more everything than anyone else at Chilleen. She's the star of the gymnastics team. Some people say she's good enough for all-state." Monica's heart sank.

They watched while Bridget—perfectly and effort-lessly—performed the same moves that Monica had just done. She paused a moment before beginning the vault and stared directly at Monica, her expression seeming to say, "This is how it is done." Then she ran, leaped over the horse, and landed in a perfect dismount.

"Wow!" said Monica, her dreams of being the gymnas-tics star disappearing.

"Bridget's just wonderful," said Kim. "But you're as good as she is—in some of the things. I saw her watching you on the parallel bars, and she didn't look happy. You did better than I've ever seen her do."

"Thanks for saying so," said Monica.

Another girl began her routines as Bridget walked over to the bleachers to join some girls sitting up a few rows from Monica and Kim.

"So," said Kim, "how was your first night in the haunted room?"

"No ghosts," said Monica, laughing. "But I found the strangest thing." She told Kim about the doll and how she had found it.

"You mean it was hidden in that spooky old closet since Allegra Chilleen lived in the room?"

"Could have been, for all I know," said Monica. "There was so much dust that that compartment couldn't have been opened in years."

"Wow," said Kim. "Are you going to tell Mrs. Danita about it? It probably belongs to the school."

"I don't know. I thought about telling her, but that would mean giving up the doll. Maybe I'll tell her at the end of the semester."

"Just make sure she doesn't see it," said Kim. "I wonder how it got into that secret compartment."

"I haven't a clue, but I'm glad it was there. You'll have to come look at it."

"I'd love to, Monica. In fact, how about right after practice?"

"You're going to play with dolls after practice?" said a mocking voice behind them. "How cute."

Both girls spun around to see Bridget sitting on the bleacher right behind them.

"Bridget!" said Kim. "How long have you been there?"

"Long enough," said Bridget. "Long enough to hear all about her haunted room and the mysterious doll."

"Well, if you're interested, I'd be happy to tell you all about it," said Monica, stung and embarrassed. "You don't have to eavesdrop."

For a moment Bridget had no reaction—she was so surprised by Monica's statement. Finally the corners of her mouth turned up and she smiled nastily. But when she opened her mouth to speak, Kim cut her off.

"Bridget, this is Monica Case. She's a new—"

"I know who she is," said Bridget, her voice cold and mocking. "I can't believe you really buy that stuff about the room being haunted," she said directly to Monica. "And getting all excited over a doll? How can you be such a baby?"

Monica just stared at Bridget. What in the world did Bridget have against her?

"She's probably just jealous because you're so good in gymnastics," Kim was saying. The girls were in Monica's room. Kim was examining the doll, turning it over in her hands as they talked.

"But she's better than I am," Monica protested. "It's not like I'm a major threat to her or anything."

"You're the closest thing to a threat she has," said Kim. "And who knows? With more practice you could probably be as good as she is." She stood up, setting the doll back on Monica's bureau. "This doll is really great," she said. "Don't worry about Bridget. She's basically a snobby jerk. She thinks because she has so much money, she's better than everyone else."

"Well, thanks," said Monica, following her new friend to the door. "I just hope she doesn't say anything about the doll."

"See you tomorrow," said Kim. Monica waved, said good-bye, and closed the door. Then she sat at her desk and opened her history book. She tried to study, but couldn't get her mind off Bridget and her nasty remarks.

Kim thinks I'm nearly as good as Bridget, she thought. *And maybe I am, and maybe that's why Bridget was so nasty to me. I know I need more practice, but what if I could show her up eventually?* She closed her eyes and imagined herself doing a series of perfect flips and perfect vaults. Then she imagined the disappointed and angry look on Bridget's face when she realized Monica was better than she was.

Feeling better, she opened her eyes. At a soft sound, she turned toward the bureau. The doll was sitting where Kim had left it. Its wide eyes stared down at Monica, but they were no longer china blue. Instead, they were red—the same glowing red color she had seen coming from the closet the night before!

CHAPTER 4

MONICA yawned and closed her history book long past lights-out. She was exhausted and thought she'd sleep like a rock. It was two weeks into the semester, and she still wasn't used to all the work. Between gymnastics practice and schoolwork, she had almost no free time and had to work late into the night to catch up.

She crawled into bed and closed her eyes, but sleep didn't come. Her mind was racing, and she felt wide-awake and restless. There were too many things to think about. In only two weeks at Chilleen she had met so many new people and learned so much. She and Kim had both made the gymnastics team, and practice was the high point of every day for them. Almost everyone she met was friendly—everyone but Bridget.

Why is she so hostile? Monica wondered for the hundredth time. Bridget was nearly perfect in gymnastics— the best on the team—but she saw Monica as a threat. She never missed an opportunity to say something sarcastic about Monica or the doll.

Monica glanced at the bureau. In the dark she could just make out the outline of the doll as it sat leaning against the wall. Remembering how its eyes had seemed to glow red on that first day made a shiver run up the back of her neck.

Don't be ridiculous, she told herself. *You just imagined the eyes were red. Besides, the doll can't see anything. It's just a doll.*

But once Monica had the idea in her mind, she couldn't get rid of it. She felt that the doll was staring directly at her—as if it expected something from her.

Taking a deep breath, Monica rolled onto her back, closed her eyes, and tried to do some relaxing exercises. Was the doll still staring? Were its eyes glowing red again? Her eyes snapped open and she sat straight up in bed.

"I'll never get to sleep!" she said aloud. She threw off the covers, padded over to the bureau, and turned the doll around. "Stare at the wall!" she told it. "I'm going to sleep."

She climbed back into bed and fluffed up her pillow. Finally she did begin to relax, and was on the edge of deep sleep when a sudden noise, no more than a rustling, made her open her eyes again. Nothing seemed different. Monica was about to dismiss the noise when she glanced at the bureau.

She couldn't believe what she saw. Standing to the side of the bureau was the shimmering profile of a young girl dressed in a long dress and high-topped leather boots. She had a dainty, pretty face, marred only by a heart-shaped birthmark on her right cheek. Her brown hair was gathered up in a loose knot, and she was standing on tiptoe, staring up at the doll. She had an intense expression on her almost transparent face.

Monica realized then that she could see the bureau and the doll *through* the girl. Her heart began to pound in her chest.

She blinked, hoping that maybe the moonlight was playing tricks on her. But when she opened her eyes, the girl was still there, reaching for the doll longingly.

I'm dreaming, Monica tried to tell herself. But she knew she was wide-awake—awake and in the presence of a ghost.

The ghost-girl turned slowly from the doll and stared directly at Monica. Her dark eyes seemed to burn right through Monica's skin.

"Who are you?" Monica demanded in a voice she wished were stronger. "What are you doing in my room?"

The ghost-girl didn't answer or change expression. She just moved closer to Monica, beckoning to her with her hand.

Monica froze. "What do you want?" she asked, her voice shaking. She studied her room, hoping to find a place to escape or hide. But the only thing she could think of was going out the door, and that would mean having to pass the ghost.

The ghost-girl beckoned again, but this time began to back away from the dresser. Monica breathed a sigh of relief as the girl floated toward the doorway. But then she stopped and again beckoned to Monica.

"You want me to follow you?" Monica guessed as the ghost moved toward the small closet.

In answer, the ghost-girl beckoned yet again. Her outline wavered and disappeared for a moment. Then it reappeared brighter than ever.

Very slowly, Monica sat up. She'd never been so frightened in her life—but she'd never been so curious either. If she didn't follow the ghost, she wouldn't know what the girl would do next. What did the beautiful ghost-girl want? she wondered.

The door to the hall silently swung open, and the girl disappeared into the hall. She obviously wanted Monica to follow.

"Wait for me!" Monica called, quickly slipping out of bed. She hurried toward the doorway and decided to follow the ghost—wherever she was leading.

CHAPTER 5

EXCITED and terrified, Monica followed the girl to the landing at the top of the stairs. She could see the girl's feet moving, but the movements were so smooth, she seemed to be gliding rather than walking. They went slowly down the stairs and through the downstairs hall to the dayroom. From time to time the ghost's outline would fade, and Monica would wonder if she was imagining the whole thing and would wake up in bed soon.

I'm crazy, Monica thought. *This can't really be happening!*

By now the ghost had reached the front door of the academy. The door swung open on its own, letting in a blast of chilly night air and making the invitation to follow all the more obvious. The ghost-girl beckoned to Monica and then drifted out through the passageway and into the night.

Where is she taking me? Monica wondered. *What does she want?*

The girl led her across the broad wooden porch to the damp, grassy lawn, and then through an empty field toward the woods. Above them the half-moon shone icy bright, and all around, the trees sighed and moaned in the wind.

At the edge of the pine forest, the ghost-girl stopped. Monica wondered if the dark, forbidding woods were as threatening to the ghost as they were to her. But then the girl continued forward into the forest and signaled to Monica to follow with greater urgency than before. At the same time, Monica thought she felt a gentle push at her back, as if a breeze were urging her forward. And she knew that no matter how much she resisted, she couldn't stop herself from walking straight into the woods.

The moonlight filtered in through the trees, throwing soft, liquid shadows across Monica's path. The ghost-girl was moving faster now, and Monica had to hurry to keep up. It was hard to avoid tripping on the exposed tree roots and underbrush. The pine needles were springy and prickly under her feet. Somewhere overhead an owl hooted mournfully.

All of a sudden an icy chill ran through Monica's body. The ghost-girl had disappeared. Monica tore ahead, checking in all directions, desperately hoping to see the pale outline of the girl. But she was nowhere in sight.

Monica looked around and found herself in a clearing bathed in silvery light. The moon glinted on large, irregular-shaped objects. Monica peered at the closest one and realized with a shudder that it was a gravestone. Chiseled into its face was a single word: CHILLEEN.

Monica shivered as she realized she was in the Chilleen family cemetery—in the middle of the night! Was this where the ghost had meant to take her? But why? Was she the spirit of one of the dead Chilleens? Was she trying to tell this to Monica?

Monica searched for the girl with her eyes, wanting desperately to ask her. But the ghost seemed to have disappeared.

"Monica!"

At the sound of her name, Monica jumped. She whirled around and came face-to-face with Mrs. Danita.

"Monica Case!" Mrs. Danita said in a perplexed voice. She was wearing a coat over her nightgown and was holding a flashlight. "What are you doing out here? Lights-out was hours ago!"

"I—" Monica started to say, then stopped. What *was* she doing out here?

"I was following . . . following a girl," she said, pointing across the clearing, almost hoping the ghost-girl would reappear.

"What girl?" said Mrs. Danita.

"I—I thought I saw . . ." Monica trailed off, feeling foolish.

"I found the front door standing wide open," Mrs. Danita said, slipping her coat over Monica's quivering shoulders. "It's so dark out here I'm lucky I found you."

"I'm sorry," Monica said, not knowing how to explain her situation.

"Do you want to talk about it?" the woman asked gently. "We can have some hot chocolate in my office."

"No," said Monica. "Thank you. I just—I had a strange dream."

"I understand," Mrs. Danita said. "You're in a new place, and there's all the excitement of beginning the school year. No wonder you're having bad dreams."

"It wasn't *bad*, exactly." Monica stopped, not sure what else to say.

They walked the rest of the way in silence. As soon as they entered the academy, Mrs. Danita locked the door. "Are you going to be all right?" she asked, giving Monica a quick hug.

"I'm fine. I'm just sleepy."

"Then run on back to bed, Monica. Bundle up and get a good night's sleep. Everything will be okay in the morning."

"All right, Mrs. Danita. And thanks for finding me." Monica made her way through the hall and then up the stairs, feeling warm gratitude toward Mrs. Danita. She also felt very puzzled. What had really happened? Had she really seen a ghost? The old-fashioned girl had seemed so *real*—not like someone in a dream. But real girls can't fade in and out as that girl had.

Of course it wasn't a ghost, she tried to tell herself. *There are no such things as ghosts. Maybe,* she decided, *my imagination is just working overtime.*

Feeling very tired, Monica entered her room and picked up a pair of wool socks beside her bed to pull on her icy feet. She was just slipping into bed when a faint stirring caught her attention. Her eyes went right to the top of the bureau and the doll, its blue glass eyes staring down at her. Now Monica's heart began to pound as it had when she had first seen the ghost-girl.

No, she thought, *it can't be.* She stared at the doll, not wanting to believe what she saw. But there was no doubt about it. The doll was no longer facing the wall as she had placed it earlier. Now it was facing her!

CHAPTER 6

AFTER breakfast the next day, Monica had to clear the tables in the dining hall. It was her work-study job, and her partner was Jimmy, who liked to chatter while he worked. That day Monica hardly listened to a thing he said. Her mind kept running over the strange events of the previous night.

After turning the doll around for the second time the night before, Monica had finally gone back to sleep. When she got up in the morning, the doll was still facing the wall. *How could it have turned around that first time?* she wondered. *Had someone come in and moved it? Did someone know about the doll?*

"Monica!"

Monica blinked and realized that Jimmy was calling her.

"Are you going deaf?" he said. "Or are you trying to see how many dishes you can pile up before they crash to the floor?"

"I'm sorry, Jimmy," Monica said, slowly coming back to the present. She became aware then that she was holding a towering stack of dishes covered with dried egg and scraps of toast.

"Earth calling Monica!" Jimmy said in a fake alien voice.

"Monica to earth," she said, putting the dishes on the steel counter separating the kitchen from the dining hall. "Watch out for flying saucers." Going back for more dishes, she resolved to forget about the doll and the ghostly girl, and to concentrate only on school—and gymnastics.

By last period, Monica had nearly succeeded. That day's gymnastics practice was especially important. The girls were working on their routines for the first county meet, which was only two weeks away.

Kim spotted Monica through all her routines. Ms. Potter's approving smile made Monica feel confident during her best events—the balance beam and floor exercise. But when she got to the vault she barely cleared the horse and then stumbled on her dismount. Her second try was even worse. The more she tried to relax and do better, the more she tensed up.

When Monica finished practicing, she spotted Kim. Then the two girls took a break and sat on the bleachers to watch their teammates practice. "You're definitely the best," Kim assured Monica as they watched. "Except for you-know-who."

As she was saying that, they watched Bridget stumble during her floor routine. Monica couldn't help smiling to herself, but everything else Bridget did was flawless. Before doing the vault, Bridget turned to the bleachers and stared directly at Monica. Monica quickly turned her head, pretending she hadn't been watching Bridget.

30

I wish I could vault, Monica thought. *I wish I could somehow beat Bridget in the county competition.* Her eyes moved back to Bridget. And then, just as Bridget executed a perfect landing, Monica had a sudden image of the doll—its eyes glowing red.

"Whoa!" said Kim, nudging her. "Are you all right?"

"I'm fine," said Monica. "I just had the strangest thought about—about something that happened last night."

"More spooky stuff in your room? What else happened? Tell me about it!"

Monica looked around to make sure Bridget couldn't overhear them. But Bridget was still down on the floor. She told Kim about the ghostly girl visitor and how the doll had seemed to move.

"Wow," said Kim, her round face showing her excitement. "I'm beginning to think that wing of the academy really *is* haunted."

Monica shrugged. "I'd think so, too, except I don't believe in ghosts."

"Me, neither," said Kim. "Not really. But what if the girl really *was* a ghost? Maybe all she wanted was the doll."

"What do you mean?"

"Well, if the doll is as old as you think, Mon, maybe it belonged to the girl before she was a ghost. Maybe she wants the doll back."

Monica laughed. "Kim, what would a ghost do with a doll?"

"I don't know. But if she wants it, maybe you ought to let her have it. I don't know, maybe you should give it to Mrs. Danita and let the school deal with it."

"But I want to keep it," Monica protested. "It's really unusual. I want to see if I can find out about its history."

"You could find out about its history without keeping it."

"But it's an antique, and I *want* it."

"But something about it gives me the creeps," said Kim. "And even if the ghost was only a dream, it might mean something. Keeping that doll could end up causing you a lot of trouble."

Monica practiced so hard for the gymnastics meet that she nearly forgot about the doll and her mysterious visitor. With Kim's help she spent every spare minute practicing her vault. When she relaxed she could do it perfectly, but as soon as she thought of Bridget she'd feel herself tense up, lose confidence, and blow it.

Finally the day of the county meet arrived and the girls were on the bus to Silverbell. Monica tried deep breathing to relax, but it didn't help. Nothing seemed to help. "Come on, Mon, *relax*," said Kim, sitting beside her. "Just tell yourself how good you are."

"Except in the vault," said Monica gloomily.

"So what? You're in the running for individual prizes in all the other events."

"You really think so?" Monica asked.

"Sure I do," said Kim. "The only other Chilleen girl who has a chance is Bridget."

Feeling better, Monica followed her friend off the bus and into the big Silverbell High School gym. Her palms were sweaty and her heart was beating rapidly, which always happened to her before big meets. The gym seemed too bright and too noisy, but she blocked it out as best she could.

"Final run-throughs," announced Ms. Potter. "Monica, you and Bridget work together on the vault. Donna and Tracy, the two of you should practice the uneven parallel bars. . . ."

Monica walked over to where Bridget was standing by the horse as Ms. Potter continued to rattle off names.

"This is your first county meet?" Bridget said, doing stretches on the horse.

"Yes," said Monica, relieved that Bridget was being nice.

"Don't worry," Bridget said. "I'm sure you'll do fine." She gave Monica a friendly wink before stepping back to prepare for a practice run. Monica watched as she sprinted up to the beat board, cartwheeled in midair, and landed on her hands in the center of the horse. But just as she began to flip into her dismount, something went wrong.

Instead of the perfect, smooth landing Bridget had done so many times, her body suddenly shifted off balance, and as Monica watched in horror, Bridget fell, landing on her arm and screaming in pain.

CHAPTER 7

"**O**H!" Bridget cried. "My wrist, my wrist!"

Her heart thudding, Monica knelt down beside Bridget, who was cradling her wrist and sobbing. Her hand was bent at an unnatural angle.

Ms. Potter nudged Monica aside as someone came running with a stretcher. To her relief, Monica saw Bridget move her arm and say something to Ms. Potter.

"Don't try to move," Ms. Potter ordered. "Everything will be all right."

A few minutes later an ambulance came and took Bridget to Silverbell Hospital emergency room. Mr. Meyers, the Chilleen volleyball coach, who had come to watch the meet, went with her, because Ms. Potter had to stay with the team. As soon as Bridget left, Ms. Potter put her arm around Monica.

"Don't feel bad, dear," she said. "It wasn't your fault. It was an accident, and there was no way you could have prevented it—even though you were spotting her. There was nothing you could have done."

"Is she going to be okay?" Monica asked.

Ms. Potter frowned. "Her wrist may be broken. If it is, she won't be able to compete for a while." Patting Monica briskly on the shoulder, she said, "I guess it's up to you now. You're our second best gymnast."

For some reason, instead of putting pressure on Monica, Ms. Potter's words relaxed her. *Without Bridget to worry about, you can be the best*, said a voice in her head. And she knew it was true.

Monica waited for her events, feeling as if she were in a dream. Before each of her routines, she could *see* herself competing and *see* herself doing her very best. It was as if all her wishes had come true.

First was the vault.

If only I don't blow this, she thought. But instead of being nervous, she was confident and certain that she would succeed.

She ran forward, flipped, pushed off the horse, and then, before she could even think, landed in a perfect dismount. Minutes later she heard the judges rank her: second. Second in the vault, her worst event! Not bad!

After that it was easy.

The second event was the uneven parallel bars. Monica felt weightless as she went through her routine. Even the hardest twists suddenly seemed easy. She wasn't surprised when the judge ranked her first. Next, she took first in the balance beam. And finally, another first, in the floor routine.

One second, three firsts. She couldn't believe it until she heard it announced that she was first overall.

"You've won!" Kim screamed in her ear. "You're number one at the whole meet!" The other girls on the team jumped and screamed and hugged her. Ms. Potter was hugging her, too. "We're so proud of you, Monica," she said. "Your scores are the best a Chilleen girl has ever gotten in a countywide meet!"

"Really?" Monica was grinning so hard, her face actually hurt.

"Really!" repeated Ms. Potter. "And of course, you've got the top spot on the team now."

As she rode on the bus back to the academy, Monica couldn't stop thinking about the past few hours. Number one in the meet, number one on the team. When they reached the school, everyone scrambled off the bus and took off for their rooms.

"Well, you did it," said Kim, patting Monica on the back. "See you tomorrow. My dad's waiting for me in his van."

" 'Bye, Kim," said Monica absentmindedly, drinking in the chill night air. *I won*, she thought over and over. *I won*, she thought as she climbed the stairs to her room. *I won*.

She unpacked her gym bag and stowed it in the closet. When she crossed to the bureau to get her nightgown, her eyes fell on the doll. A wave of terror tore through her body. The doll's eyes were glowing bright red again.

Then she noticed something else—the doll's necklace, which she hadn't really looked at since that morning when she found the doll. The reflection from the red eyes made the necklace glow now. Monica took a closer look at it and felt a sudden chill.

"All Your Wishes," the words on the necklace said.

Suddenly an overwhelming sense of guilt came over her. *Does this mean I could have caused Bridget's accident?*

She continued to stare at the doll's glowing red eyes and the strange message around its neck.

"All your wishes," she whispered. "All my wishes have come true."

CHAPTER 8

MONICA waved at three kids she knew from Spanish class as she rushed to the gym a few days later. It seemed as if she knew practically everyone in school now—and they knew her. Part of it was winning the county gymnastics meet. But it was also, Monica realized, because she was happy and everyone could tell.

Kim greeted her outside the locker room. "I'm having a skating party for my birthday on Saturday," she said. "I'd love it if you could come."

"Sounds great," said Monica.

"It's at Skateworld," Kim went on. "They've got colored lights and great music. And then afterward I thought you could come home with me and spend the night."

"I'd love to. I'll just have to get permission from Mrs. Danita."

"Good. It's settled. I guess I'm pretty lucky to have the most popular girl at school come to my party," Kim added mischievously.

"Give me a break," said Monica.

"Well, now that you won the competition, everyone wants to know you. And, by the way, guess who's back at school?"

Monica felt her heart sink. "Bridget?" she guessed. "How's she doing?"

"She's fine. Except she has to wear a cast for a few weeks. But I hear she isn't too happy about losing first place on the team."

"I don't blame her. I still feel really bad about what happened. I keep thinking that maybe I can make it up to her some way."

"Well, here's your chance."

Monica followed Kim's gaze and saw Bridget and her roommate, Peggy, coming toward them. As usual, Bridget was dressed in expensive clothes, a cashmere sweater over designer jeans. Her left arm was in a sling made from a flowered silk scarf, and she had a soft leather jacket draped over her shoulders.

Bridget was laughing at something Peggy had said, but as soon as she saw Monica, her smile disappeared.

"Hi, Bridget," Monica said, trying to sound cheerful and friendly. "How are you feeling?"

"I'm fine," said Bridget, her expression cold. Before Monica could think of what to say next, Kim spoke up.

"Great jacket, Bridget," she said.

Bridget's face relaxed in a smile. "My parents got it for me while I was in the hospital."

"It's really beautiful," said Monica, still trying to be friendly. "And it goes perfectly with your outfit."

"Do you really think so?" Bridget said, staring directly at Monica.

"I love it," said Monica, relieved that Bridget was at

39

least talking to her. "I always wished I could have one like it, but they're too expensive for me."

Bridget's expression changed again. "Oh, is that right?" she said. "Well, I guess you can't have *everything* you want."

"What do you mean?" said Monica, surprised by Bridget's nasty tone of voice.

"I mean that you already got what you wanted most." And Bridget tapped her right hand on the cast.

Monica was horrified at what she was hearing. "Bridget, that's not true! I feel terrible about your accident!"

"Sure you do. Except with me off the team, you made first place. You're *glad* I was hurt, Monica; why don't you just admit it?"

"Bridget, I—"

Bridget, her pretty face twisting with anger and jealousy, cut Monica off. "I know what you're thinking. You think you can be nice to me and I'll forget what you did. Well, it won't work, Monica. I know what you're up to, and I'm going to make sure everybody else knows, too!"

Gathering her jacket around her shoulders, Bridget pushed between Monica and Kim and went down the hall. Peggy stood still a moment, obviously embarrassed. Then she whispered a quick " 'Bye," and hurried after her friend.

Monica stood staring after Bridget in anger and dismay.

"Come on, Monica." Kim put an arm around her friend's shoulder. "Don't pay any attention to Bridget. I told you she's a jerk."

"But she thinks I wanted her to fall. And she's telling everyone—"

"No one will believe her," said Kim. "What could you

have done to hurt her? Let's have a great time this weekend and forget all about Bridget."

By Sunday afternoon Monica had almost forgotten the
incident with Bridget. The skating party had been fun,
and so had the rest of the weekend. The girls had spent all
day Sunday eating homemade food and watching videos.

"Your mom is a great cook," she told Kim, folding a
shirt into her overnight case. "I can't believe she makes
pizza from scratch."

"I know," said Kim, flopping down on her bed. "She
makes all kinds of great things. She says it's because she
likes to eat so much." She watched Monica for a moment.
"I've had the most wonderful birthday weekend," she
said. "Did you have a good time?"

"I had a great time! But it went by too fast. Both your
parents are so nice. In fact, your dad reminds me of my
dad."

"Really?"

"Yeah. I hate to admit it," Monica went on, "but being
here has made me miss my family—even my baby sister."

Kim was sympathetic. "I'd hate to be away from my
folks," she admitted.

"On the other hand, I *love* Chilleen," Monica said.

"Well, you're invited to come home with me any time
you want." Kim lay back on the pillows and held her
wrist up in the air. "I just love my new bracelet," she
said. She turned her arm and admired the delicate silver
bracelet her parents had given her for her birthday. It was
a Navajo design, inset with alternating circles of turquoise
and mother-of-pearl.

"It's beautiful," Monica agreed. "I've got a sweater that would go with it perfectly. Want to borrow it?"

"Sure," said Kim. "Thanks. And I love the sweatshirt you got me."

"All aboard!" Kim's father's voice boomed from downstairs.

"Come on," said Kim. "Dad's ready to take you back to school. I'll ride along to keep you company."

"Good. I can give you the sweater then."

On the drive back to school, Kim told her dad about an English paper she was working on while Monica gazed out the window. The valley was beautiful with its thick pine forest, red rocks, and rugged purple mountains below the western sky. It was close to sunset when the dark bulk of the academy loomed up in front of them.

"Look!" said Kim. Monica followed Kim's finger to a point high above the academy where a hawk circled. Only in the West, she thought.

Kim went upstairs with Monica so she could get the sweater. "I guess the ghost didn't come back to get her doll," Kim observed as they entered the room.

"Will you stop that?" said Monica, laughing. "I told you, the ghost was just a dream."

"More like a nightmare." Kim idly picked up the doll and turned it over in her hands. "It's just so strange," she said. "Imagine its being locked away in that closet all those years."

"I know," said Monica, handing Kim a pretty beige sweater.

"Thanks." Kim replaced the doll on the bureau. "This is lovely," she said, admiring the sweater. "I guess I better go. See you tomorrow—and thanks for coming for my birthday."

"Thank *you*," said Monica. "It was really great. And tell your mom—"

At that moment there was a knock on the door. Kim, who was closest, opened it.

Surprised, the two girls saw Mrs. Danita standing there with Bridget. There was something very wrong with Bridget. Her usually pretty and delicate features were red and puffy. Before Monica could say anything, Bridget pointed her finger at Monica and began shouting.

"*She* took it!" she said. "She's a thief!"

CHAPTER 9

"IT was her!" Bridget said, close to hysteria. "She stole it! She's the one!"

"Stole what?" said Monica, bewildered. "What are you talking about?"

"That's it, play innocent!" said Bridget. "But you aren't going to get away—"

"Bridget, please!" said Mrs. Danita sharply. Looking as if she had been slapped, Bridget stopped shouting, but she continued to glare at Monica.

"I'm sorry about this, Monica," Mrs. Danita apologized. "Bridget's new leather jacket is missing—"

"And Monica stole it!" Bridget interjected. "She caused my accident, and now she stole my leather jacket."

"Bridget, be quiet!" Mrs. Danita said. "If you don't quiet down, I'll have to ask you to wait downstairs." Appearing more embarrassed than ever, Mrs. Danita forced herself to continue. "Now, I'm certainly not accusing you of anything, Monica, but Bridget is convinced that—that you took her jacket."

"What? I *never!*" cried Monica, horrified. "How could anyone think such a thing?"

"I told you *I'm* not accusing you," Mrs. Danita said. "But Bridget made the accusations, and I felt it was best to confront you with . . ." An odd expression came over Mrs. Danita's face.

"What a nice doll." She walked over to the bureau, picked up the doll, and asked, "Is this from your childhood?"

For a moment Monica was speechless. "I—I really haven't had it that long," she said, not daring to meet Kim's eyes.

"It's a beautiful antique," said Mrs. Danita. "I wonder how old it—"

"Who cares about the doll!" said Bridget. "She took my jacket."

Mrs. Danita shot her a look of disapproval, which quieted her down.

Monica's cheeks burned with indignation, but at the same time she felt cold inside—cold with anger. She glanced around the room at her visitors. Mrs. Danita seemed to be embarrassed, Bridget was smirking, and Kim appeared bewildered and slightly frightened. Only the doll, which Mrs. Danita had put back on the bureau, had its usual stony expression and stared at Monica with its pale blue eyes.

Monica took a deep breath. "I didn't take Bridget's jacket, Mrs. Danita," she said as calmly as she could. "I haven't even seen it since the day she wore it to school. If you don't believe me, you're welcome to search my room."

"I'm sure that won't be necessary," said Mrs. Danita.

"Go on!" said Monica. "Take a look!"

Mrs. Danita halfheartedly opened and shut the closet door. "Come on, Bridget," she urged. "There's no sign of the jacket here. And Monica has denied—"

"She's a liar!" cried Bridget. "She took it! I know she did!" She began to open and close drawers, checking under piles of sweaters and T-shirts. She yanked open the closet door and began to rummage through Monica's clothes.

"That's enough, Bridget," said Mrs. Danita. "Now, come on."

"Oh, let her look," said Monica. "I don't have anything to hide. There's no leather jacket in there."

"Then what's *this?*" cried Bridget, emerging from the closet. In her hand was the leather jacket hanging from a padded satin hanger.

"See?" Bridget turned to Mrs. Danita, who was now frowning. "I *told* you she took it!"

"Well, Monica," the older woman said, sounding perplexed. "Can you explain this?"

For a moment Monica thought she must be having a nightmare. This couldn't be happening. But the tone of disappointment in Mrs. Danita's voice convinced her that it was real.

Monica stared at Mrs. Danita. "No," she whispered. "I don't have any idea how the jacket got in my closet, but I promise you I did not put it there. I didn't take it, Mrs. Danita; please believe me."

Mrs. Danita slowly shook her head. "I don't know what to believe," she said, obviously upset.

"Believe she's a thief!" said Bridget. "My jacket was in her closet, Mrs. Danita."

"I'm going to get to the bottom of this," Mrs. Danita said, "but this isn't the time or the place. Monica, see me in my office tomorrow morning. Bridget, come on."

With a self-satisfied smile, Bridget followed the woman out, clutching her jacket.

After they had gone, Monica leaned against the door in despair. "I don't believe this!"

"Me neither," said Kim.

"I didn't take the jacket!"

"I know you didn't. I know you would never do anything like that. But . . ." Kim's voice trailed off.

"But how did it get in my closet? I can't even imagine."

"I know," said Kim suddenly. "Maybe Bridget put it there herself when you were gone this weekend—to get you in trouble. In fact, that must be what happened."

"Maybe." But deep down Monica didn't believe that anyone—even Bridget—would do anything so spiteful.

"You'll see," said Kim. "I don't know how, but somehow I'm going to prove that Bridget, or her drippy roommate, Peggy, did this."

Monica thanked her, but she felt so awful, she didn't have much hope that Kim could prove anything.

Outside Monica's window a horn sounded.

"Oops, that must be my dad. I've got to go." Kim gave Monica a quick hug. "Try not to worry, Mon," she said. "I'll see you tomorrow."

Monica walked over to the window and watched as her friend ran out the back door and climbed into her father's blue van. She continued to watch as the van drove down the red dirt road and disappeared around the bend toward town. Though there was a beautiful sunset, Monica barely noticed it. All she could think about was the jacket. How had it gotten in her closet?

Had Bridget or her roommate planted it there? Or was there some other explanation?

Monica turned back to the room and saw that the doll's eyes were glowing red. Monica closed her own eyes. "I am imagining this," she said aloud. "I must be." And to her relief, when she opened her eyes the doll's eyes were their usual shade of blue. And the message on the doll's necklace was the same: "All Your Wishes."

CHAPTER 10

THE next morning Monica wasn't surprised when Mrs. Danita informed her that she was on probation. She could see the pain in Mrs. Danita's eyes and knew the headmistress felt terrible about it too. But, as she told Monica, she felt she had "no choice."

Feeling as if she were inside a dark cloud, Monica left the office. How could this have happened to her? She hadn't done anything wrong, and now she was on probation. If anything else went wrong, she could get kicked out of school.

For the next few days she continued to move around in her cloud. She avoided Bridget as much as possible. This was pretty easy even in gymnastics since Bridget had to sit on the sidelines till her wrist was healed.

Kim did everything she could to cheer up Monica, and eventually it did begin to work. Monica did feel better. It was partly knowing she had such a good friend, and partly because she had gotten even busier with schoolwork. She didn't have time to think of other things. Midterms were coming up in a few weeks. She had to study for exams in math and Spanish, write a long essay in English, and write a paper for history. Mr. Taylor, the history teacher, said the paper had to be on an aspect of regional history.

"I'm going to do my paper on the first continental railroad," Kim told Monica.

"Did the railroad go through here?" asked Monica.

"It went through one edge of Phantom Valley. And besides, my great-great-grandfather worked on it."

"That sounds interesting." But Monica was barely listening as Kim went on to talk about her family and the railroad. Kim had just given her an idea.

"Mon? What are you going to write yours on?"

"The Chilleen family," Monica said. As she said it, she realized that the topic would be perfect.

"The Chilleens!" Kim stared at her as if she had announced she was going to write about flying saucers landing in Phantom Valley. "But they weren't famous."

"They're an important part of *local* history," said Monica. "The Chilleens helped settle Phantom Valley. Besides, I want to find out more about Allegra, and this is the perfect chance."

"Because you're living in her room?"

"Well, partly," Monica admitted. "And also, I have a feeling that all the spooky stuff with the doll and the ghost has something to do with the Chilleen family."

After gymnastics practice Monica went to the school library, which was on the top floor of the wing opposite the wing her room was in. Every time Monica entered the library, she felt thrilled by the huge old room with its vaulted windows, shiny wooden bookcases, and musty, dusty smells.

The polished wood paneling was lined with photographs and portraits. In the photographs she recognized the academy building from the days when it was newer and smaller. Over the years she could see the building grow as new wings and outbuildings were added. The portraits of men, women, and children from the 1800s were hung along one wall.

"Are any of these people Chilleens?" she asked the librarian.

The librarian, a pleasant gray-haired woman named Ms. Martin, removed her glasses and blew on the lenses before polishing them on a Kleenex. "Yes, they're all members of the Chilleen family," she said. "This was once their family home, you know."

"I know," said Monica. She walked slowly along the wall, taking in the images of the dozens of departed Chilleens. Fascinated, she read the names: Ebenezer, Aldrich, Ramona, Cuthbert . . . *They're all cool names*, she thought. *But where is Allegra?* Then she remembered that Allegra had been a member of the last Chilleen family to live there. She walked to the end of the informal portrait gallery, where the photos, though still old, were newer and more modern than the others. Here she found a group of family portraits. The parents—Valentine and Morgana— were in the top row, and below them were portraits of four children: Jeb, Prudence, Hortensia, Ambey, but no Allegra. Next to the portrait of Ambey, a serious-looking young boy with dark, curly hair, was a faded rectangle on the wall. A faded rectangle the size of a small picture.

Monica was certain that the missing photo had to be

Allegra's. But where was it? And why had it been removed?

"Excuse me," she said, approaching the librarian again. "Are there any other pictures of the Chilleens here? Or any information about them?"

"Why, yes," said Ms. Martin, again removing her reading glasses. "There's a large drawer filled with family papers locked away in the stacks. And let me think—yes, there's a book that was privately printed about fifty years ago, detailing the history of the Chilleens and some of the other pioneer families in Phantom Valley. Let me just look. . . ."

Ms. Martin got up from her desk and moved a sliding wooden ladder along a tall bookcase. She climbed the ladder and reached up to the highest shelf for a thick, dusty green book. "Here you are," she said, climbing down the ladder and handing the book to Monica.

"Thanks," said Monica. The cover was faded, but she could easily make out the title: *The Pioneers of Phantom Valley*.

She took the book to a table and began to leaf through it. The first half of the book was all about the geography and history of Phantom Valley. There were chapters on agriculture, mining, and the Native Americans who had lived there earlier. The first family to come to the valley had been named Bendigo, but they had soon been followed by the Chilleens.

Monica eagerly flipped through the chapter about the Chilleens. She learned that Phantom Valley had been partially settled by Ebenezer Chilleen and his six brothers. There were more than a dozen old photos and drawings from the 1860s showing the ancient Native American village in the cliffs, a small settlement of log cabins, and men and women clearing land and planting crops. There were more pictures of old Ebenezer Chilleen and his many children, nieces, and nephews than there had been on the wall. The pictures were arranged chronologically throughout the chapter—the most recent ones being near the end of it.

As she turned over the last page, Monica felt as if her heart had stopped beating. There, in the bottom center of the page, was a photograph of a young girl dressed in a high-collared dress, holding a doll. The girl was slim and dark, with thick dark hair pulled back on the sides. On her right cheek, barely visible, was a birthmark in the shape of a heart.

It was the same girl Monica had seen in her room, but this one wasn't a ghost. And the doll was the same one that was now sitting on Monica's dresser. The caption under the picture identified the girl as Allegra Chilleen.

But on the photograph itself someone had written: "The Evil One."

CHAPTER 11

FOR a long moment Monica stared at the stiffly posed photograph of the solemn girl. Allegra. Allegra Chilleen. The girl who had once lived in Monica's room. The ghost who had come into the room a few weeks ago.

Monica *hadn't* dreamt it. The ghost girl had been real. But what had she wanted? And why would someone call Allegra "The Evil One"?

I've got to find out more about the Chilleens, Monica thought. *I have to find out why Allegra came into my room.*

"Well," said Ms. Martin when Monica returned the book. "Did you find everything you wanted?"

"I got a good start," said Monica. "But I need more information. May I see the papers in the stacks?"

"I'm sorry, but the stacks are locked. You'll need to get written permission from a teacher."

"No problem. I'm sure my history teacher will sign. I'm researching a history paper."

"The Chilleen family is an interesting topic," said Ms. Martin.

"It is." *More than you can imagine,* Monica thought.

She gathered up her books and headed for the library door. At the doorway someone carrying a load of books in one arm came hurrying in without looking and ran right into Monica. The person staggered forward and books were scattered everywhere.

"Excuse me!" said Monica.

"My fault," said a familiar voice. Monica saw that it was Bridget who had fallen against her. At the same time Bridget recognized Monica, and her expression changed from friendly to cold. "I might have known," she said. "Who else is always getting in my way?"

"*You* ran into *me,*" Monica pointed out.

"What are *you* doing here?" asked Bridget. "Don't tell me you're taking precious time away from gymnastics to study."

Bridget's sarcasm made Monica feel defensive. *Be nice to her,* she reminded herself. *Give her a chance.* "As a matter of fact," Monica said, trying to sound friendlier than she felt, "I'm studying. I'm researching a history paper on the Chilleens."

"The *Chilleens?*" Bridget stared at her.

"It's all part of the pioneer history of Phantom Valley," Monica went on. "I happen to find it interesting."

"Right," said Bridget. "Whatever turns you on." She had finished picking up her books and, without another word, turned and walked away.

I give up, Monica thought. *I'll never make friends with her in a million years.*

Monica had just gotten back to her room when there was a knock on the door. "Who is it?" Monica called. The door burst open and Kim came in.

"Hi, Kim," said Monica. "I've got the most exciting news!"

"Really?"

Monica told her what she'd discovered in the library.

"So you mean the picture of Allegra Chilleen looked like the ghost you saw in your room?" Kim asked.

"It *was* her," said Monica. "It was the same girl."

"Whoa. Maybe you ought to change rooms."

"Are you kidding, Kim? This is really cool. Now that I know she's real, I'm going to find out what she wants."

"What do you mean, Mon?"

"I'm not sure. But somehow I have a feeling I'm getting closer to the truth—the truth about Allegra."

"The Evil One," said Kim, her smile mischievous.

"Right."

"I wonder why they called her that?" said Kim.

"I don't know."

"Too bad you can't just ask her."

Monica stared at her friend. "You know what?" she said. "Maybe I can."

After Kim left, Monica tried to study her Spanish, but it was no use. She couldn't stop thinking about Allegra. *Why didn't I think of it before?* she thought. She realized that the only time she had seen Allegra, it had been late at night. Maybe if she stayed up late again, Allegra would come back. Then she could find out what the ghost wanted.

By twelve o'clock there was still no sign of Allegra Chilleen. Monica had eaten a quick dinner and then returned to her room. She lay on her bed trying to do a math problem while she waited for the ghost. But she couldn't concentrate. She decided it was the doll on the bureau making her feel uneasy. *It's like I'm constantly being watched,* she thought. Finally she got up and picked up the doll.

"Sorry, doll," Monica said out loud, "but I have to put you away. Otherwise, I'll never get any studying done." She opened the closet door and put the doll back into the secret compartment. Feeling better, she went back to the math problem, but after only a few moments she felt her eyelids flutter. The next thing she knew, it was morning.

Monica woke up slowly, feeling confused and a little frightened. She had a vague feeling that she'd had a nightmare but couldn't remember anything about it. Yawning, she stretched and her hand bumped something that shouldn't have been there. She turned over quickly, took one look, and began to scream.

CHAPTER 12

MONICA jumped out of bed and stared down at the rumpled bedclothes. There, lying next to the pillow, was the doll.

How had it gotten there? She had put it in the secret compartment in the closet. Or had she?

Shivering, Monica glanced over at the closet. The door was open. Holding her breath, Monica walked over to the closet and peered inside. Everything was the same, but something was different—the secret door in back was hanging open.

Had Allegra's ghost taken the doll from the cubbyhole and placed it on Monica's bed? Could ghosts pick things up and carry them?

Maybe, she thought, *I sleepwalked and took the doll out myself. After all, I was thinking about it just before I fell asleep. Or maybe I'm just going crazy.*

She returned to the bed, picked up the doll, and examined it closely as she had done so many times before. Nothing was different, so she placed it on top of her bureau and made the bed. *There's got to be a logical explanation*, she thought. *There's got to be!*

After school Monica had an appointment with Mr. Taylor to discuss her paper. History had always been her favorite subject, and she was more excited about this paper than any other school project she'd ever done. And she couldn't wait to tell the teacher what she'd chosen to write about.

Even if she weren't trying to find out about Allegra, the history of the Chilleen family would have been interesting. But with Allegra involved, the paper seemed like the most important thing in her life. Monica wanted to find out everything about Allegra and her life. Reading about the girl who had lived ninety years ago would be fascinating, and possibly, it would lead her to the reason Allegra's ghost was still haunting the school. She was determined to find this out.

Mr. Taylor was a short, soft-spoken man with a fringe of gray hair and wire-rimmed glasses. He gave Monica a small smile and invited her to sit down. The office was tiny, and every square inch of wall space was covered with bookshelves that were jammed with thick old volumes. Behind his desk, a small window looked out on the grounds and pine forest.

"Well, Miss Case," Mr. Taylor said pleasantly. "Have you given any thought to the topic of your research paper?"

"I know exactly what I want to do," Monica said. "In fact, I've already started working on it."

"Well, that's splendid. You'd be surprised how many students claim they can't find a topic. I can never understand this, since we live in a world of hundreds of exciting subjects."

"I'll need you to sign a library pass, Mr. Taylor. I have to get into the stacks for my research."

"I'm sure that won't be a problem. But you haven't yet told me your topic."

"Oh, sorry. I'm just so excited about it. I want to research the history of the Chilleen family."

Now Mr. Taylor's expression changed to dismay. "Did you say the Chilleens?"

"Yes. Is there something wrong with that? It's a perfect topic. They were one of the original families to settle Phantom Valley, and they gave the land and original building for the school—"

"Yes, yes, I know all that," Mr. Taylor interrupted. "It's a splendid idea, but I'm afraid it's already been taken. This morning Miss Morgan told me that *she's* doing *her* paper on the Chilleens."

Monica couldn't believe her ears. "Miss Morgan?"

"Bridget Morgan," he said. "How extraordinary that two of you should have chosen the same topic."

"She stole my idea!" Monica blurted out.

Mr. Taylor frowned. "Now, Miss Case, I wouldn't go making accusations—"

"She did! I told her about it in the library yesterday. She pretended she wasn't interested. Then she went and stole it!"

"Well, that's between you and Miss Morgan," he said gruffly. "The fact remains that she came to me with the idea first."

"Are you saying that I can't do mine on the Chilleens, too?" Monica asked, horrified.

"I'm afraid not. You'll have to find another topic."

"But that's not fair!" Monica protested.

"Life," Mr. Taylor pronounced, "is not always fair."

"Could you at least give me a library pass?"

"We'll talk about that when you find another topic."

Just then Mrs. Douglas, another history teacher, knocked on the half-open door. "Excuse me, John," she said to Mr. Taylor, "but there's something urgent that I have to discuss with you." Noticing Monica, she said, "Excuse me, dear, but this'll take only a minute."

"What is it?" said Mr. Taylor, following the other teacher out into the hall. Before closing the door behind him, he smiled at Monica and said, "I'll be back in a minute."

Monica had never been so angry in her life. Bridget was making her life miserable. But then she spotted something on Mr. Taylor's desk. Atop a neatly stacked pile of papers was a small white memo pad. At the top was printed, "From the Desk of John Taylor, Jr."

Monica stared at the pad for a moment while a thought formed in her mind. Did she dare?

I've got to get into the stacks, she thought. *I've got to.* It would be easy to write a short note that said she was allowed in the stacks.

Monica stared at the closed door, able to hear the muffled voices of the two teachers. Quickly she tore off the top piece of memo paper and slipped it inside her notebook—just as the door opened and Mr. Taylor walked in.

"I'm sorry, Monica," said Mr. Taylor, "but I have to go to a meeting now. See me on Monday—with a new topic."

Monica left the office. Bridget had stolen her paper idea!

How could she have done such a thing? And Mr. Taylor hadn't believed her. He hadn't even seemed to care! *I wish I had a different history teacher,* she thought. *Why can't I be in Mrs. Douglas's class?*

With her heart thudding, she returned to her room and sat down at her desk, looking at the notepaper. Her hands were trembling.

Stop it, Monica! she told herself. *What you're thinking is stupid and against school rules. And wrong.*

But was it really wrong? After all, Mr. Taylor would have gladly given her a pass if Bridget hadn't stolen her research idea.

No. Stop thinking about it.

I've got to get into the stacks. I have to find out about Allegra.

For a moment Monica felt as if two separate people were arguing inside her head. *It won't hurt anybody,* she found herself thinking. *Mr. Taylor will never know.* Then, so quickly that she surprised herself, she picked up a pen. She began to write in a strong hand that didn't look anything like her handwriting—almost as if someone else were guiding the pen.

"Please allow Monica Case to use the material in the stacks. J.T.," she wrote. Monica stared at the note a moment. Then she slipped it inside her notebook and headed for the library.

CHAPTER 13

I don't believe I'm doing this, Monica thought as she stood outside the library doors. *What if Ms. Martin notices? What if I get caught? But it's the only way I'll ever find out the truth about Allegra.*

Taking a deep breath, she walked into the library and handed the forged pass to Ms. Martin. "I need to get into the stacks," she told the librarian.

Ms. Martin held the permission slip in her hand but didn't look at it. "This is for your history paper, isn't it?" she said. "Mr. Taylor?"

"That's right. I want to look at some of the private papers in there."

"Fine." Ms. Martin glanced down at the pass and frowned. "Oh," she said.

Monica felt her heart lurch in her chest. "Is something wrong?" she asked, barely able to keep her voice from shaking. *I'm going to get caught,* she thought.

"It's Mr. Taylor," said Ms. Martin. "I don't know *why* he insists on signing his initials instead of his name. I've

63

pointed out to him that there are three other faculty members with the same initials." With an annoyed frown, she impaled the permission slip on a spiked noteholder.

Monica felt relief flood through her. "Maybe he was in a hurry," she said.

"That's the trouble with everyone these days," grumbled Ms. Martin. "Always in a hurry." She reached in her top drawer and pulled out a large round key ring with a single iron key hanging from it. Then she stopped again. "Just a minute," she said abruptly.

For a moment Monica was sure her heart had stopped beating. *What now?* she thought. Did Ms. Martin realize the note was a forgery?

"Have you checked your subject in the card catalog yet?" the librarian asked.

Monica relaxed. "No, not yet."

"Better do that before you go into the stacks. The computer terminal's over there."

Monica went to the computer terminal and switched on the computerized card catalog. It seemed strange to have a modern system in such an old building.

"There's nothing under 'Chilleen' except the book you showed me," she told Ms. Martin, who was pulling a book from a nearby shelf.

"Just as I expected," said Ms. Martin. "But it's always best to check. I'm afraid most of the Chilleen things in the archives aren't cataloged."

"That's all right." Monica tried to hide her impatience. "I want to sort through things anyway."

Ms. Martin led Monica to a long, narrow room at the back of the library, which contained the stacks.

"You can work at one of those tables near the door,"

said Ms. Martin, "and, as you can see, the bookshelves are in the center. The map cases are over there, and you'll find old papers in those filing drawers along the west wall." She pointed to a bank of green filing cabinets.

Monica thanked her, put her pen and notebook down on a table, and asked, "How long can I stay?"

"I go home at six," said Ms. Martin, "but the library is open till seven. If you leave after I've gone, ask Bridget to lock up after you. She's the monitor this evening."

Monica couldn't wait for her own library work-study. It would sure beat clearing tables. But she didn't have time to think about that now. Not with the Chilleen secrets so close to being revealed.

Ms. Martin went back out into the main library and closed the door. For a moment Monica felt all alone in the old room. High above the bookshelves was an iron catwalk that ran along the back wall. Monica noticed that there would be room enough to stand on the catwalk and wondered what it was used for. She walked slowly along the bookshelves, glancing at the titles. There were rare old books on every imaginable topic, from mining claims to water rights. Finally she approached the filing cabinets. There were seven in all, and the top drawer of the one in the middle was labeled: CHILLEEN—HISTORY & MEMORABILIA.

With growing excitement, Monica opened the top drawer and found it filled with several manila file folders. She brought the folders to the table along with a sturdy cardboard filing box and sat down. Then she began to read.

Many of the papers were legal documents and land claims. There were also stacks of old letters from early

Chilleens. Fascinated, Monica read letters from old Ebenezer Chilleen to members of his family back East, telling them about the excitement and hardships of pioneer life.

The papers didn't seem to be in any particular order. Letters that were very old were in the same manila file folders as documents that were more modern. Some files contained nothing but ancient newspaper clippings about important political developments in the region, crop yields, mining claims, and unusual weather conditions.

Most of the clippings seemed to have more to do with the region itself than with the Chilleens. Monica was about to put the file back when a newspaper story caught her eye. It was from the Silverbell *Bugle,* dated October 18, 1911:

SERVICE FOR FAMILY KILLED IN FIRE

Funeral services were held today for the Valentine Chilleen family, who died from smoke inhalation on the night of October 16 when a fire was started in the sleeping wing of their sturdy frame home. The family included Valentine and his wife, Morgana, and their five children, Jeb, Prudence, Hortensia, Ambey, and Allegra. It is thought that carelessness with a kerosene lantern caused the tragic conflagration.

The article went on to describe the service and talk about how well-known the family was in the area. After she finished reading it, Monica continued to stare at the yellowing scrap of paper. The fire had taken place about eighty years ago! Had the spirit of Allegra Chilleen been haunting Phantom Valley ever since?

Next, Monica turned her attention to the cardboard filing box. As she carefully lifted the lid, crumpled bits of old paper fell onto the table. How long had it been since anyone had opened this box?

Inside were a jumble of old photographs, more letters, a plot deed for the Chilleen land, some Native American trinkets, and, bound in faded blue leather, an account book labeled HOUSEHOLD AND FARM. Monica picked up the book and flipped through the first few pages. The pale green paper was filled with columns of numbers and notations in spidery, old handwriting. They included such items as "Sacks of Feed" and payroll entries. They were, Monica realized, the accounts for the farm that had once been worked there.

There was a piece of faded ribbon stuck in the book as a bookmark. Monica turned to the page it was marking and read "Morgana Chilleen, Her Thoughts" in flowery writing.

Monica recognized the name as that of Allegra's mother. Her hands began to tremble when she realized that she was holding journal entries written by Mrs. Chilleen shortly before she and her family died in the fire. The date was late summer 1911.

Quickly Monica skimmed through the first few pages of entries. She learned that Mrs. Chilleen had confided in the diary because things were going badly on the farm, and she didn't "like to complain to my Dear Husband or Sweet Children."

Monica read about how a terrible drought had stricken Phantom Valley, causing crops to fail and animals to die. Mrs. Chilleen wrote sadly of having to let the hired men go, one by one.

On September 10, just a month before the fire, she wrote:

Today was the saddest of my life. For today my Husband told our ten remaining workers they had to go. It broke all of our hearts. Tom has worked for the family for over twenty years. Joseph has been with us almost as long, and the rest for no less than ten years—with Edward as the one exception. Edward has only been with us for two years. His past is a mystery to us. He's never been friendly, but he's always done his work. But recently he's been so silent, so apart—even angry. That is why I find it extremely odd that he was more upset than the others. I thought he'd be glad to leave here. Before he left, he gave each of the Children a Present. This was very unexpected since he almost never took notice of them. Most special was the one he gave to Allegra, being a beautiful but most peculiar Doll.

There was one more entry, in Morgana's handwriting, about the drought. "I do not know how we can go on," it read. "Things have gone from bad to worse. All I can do is pray for relief."

The entry was dated October 13. Three days later the fire had struck, killing her and her family.

Monica put down the journal. At last she knew what had happened and where the doll had come from. *Poor Mrs. Chilleen*, she thought. *I feel so sorry for her and her family.*

She put the journal and papers back in the box and replaced them in the filing drawer. Just before shutting the drawer, she noticed a small, flat box wedged in the back. Curious, she pulled it out and opened it—and found herself staring into the solemn face of Allegra Chilleen.

This was the picture missing from the wall of the library. It was the same one that had been reproduced in the book *The Pioneers of Phantom Valley*, which had been printed in the 1940s. The birthmark on her cheek was shaped exactly like a heart, and her intense dark eyes were filled with a secret sorrow. The picture was enclosed in a gilt frame with a small metal hook on the back.

I wonder why Allegra's picture isn't on the wall with the rest of her family's pictures, Monica thought. *What's her secret?*

There was something else in the box. Monica pulled it out to discover another news clipping. This one, dated October 17, 1911, was very short:

FIRE AT CHILLEEN HOUSE

Assistant Sheriff Mortimer Bendigo of Silverbell confirmed today that the tragic fire that killed the seven members of the Valentine Chilleen family was apparently set by the twelve-year-old daughter, Allegra Chilleen.

Edward Whiting, a former employee of the Chilleen family who had permission to remain in the bunkhouse told how he saw the girl, "a look of madness in her eyes," walk barefoot out to a shed. She seemed to be in a trance, he said, as she took a jar of kerosene from the shed and made her way back to the house. Whiting didn't know what she intended to do until the fire was already set and the family overcome by smoke.

Across the clipping, someone had scrawled in red ink: "The Evil One."

CHAPTER 14

MONICA glanced from the clipping to the picture of Allegra and back to the clipping again. Then she had a horrifying thought. *Allegra murdered her entire family, and now she's after me! No wonder she came into my room. I've got her doll! She wants her doll back, and I have to find a way to get it back to her!*

But how? How could she return something to a ghost?

Monica had never been so frightened in her entire life. Quickly she crammed the file folder back into the open file drawer. The bottom of the drawer was filled with loose papers and other Chilleen memorabilia, which gave her an idea. The drawer. It was the perfect place to put the doll. The doll had belonged there all along—with the rest of the Chilleen family things.

Glancing at her watch, she saw it was nearly seven! She'd have to hurry in order to make it back before the library closed. She picked up her notebook and realized she hadn't taken a single note. *Good thing I'm **not** writing my paper on this*, she thought, making sure the door to the stacks didn't lock. She raced across the library, down the stairs, across the main building, and back up the stairs to the top floor of her own wing.

Entering her room, Monica was filled with mixed emotions—fright because of what she had discovered about Allegra, but also joy and relief. She was sure that once the doll was in the drawer with the rest of the Chilleen things, Allegra would go away.

Panting, she tossed the notebook on her bed and grabbed the doll from the bureau. Her watch showed five minutes till seven.

Running back to the library, Monica had to dodge several kids on their way to dinner. "Slow down!" a boy yelled. But Monica ignored him. She got to the library with two minutes to spare.

Bridget, her back to the room, was absorbed in shelving some books. Monica tiptoed across the old wooden floor toward the stacks so as not to attract her attention. But just before she went into the stacks, Monica turned around and saw Bridget watching her. She was sure Bridget noticed the doll, too.

I can't worry about her now, Monica thought. *I've got to put the doll back where it belongs.* She was in luck—Bridget didn't come after her. She just shrugged and returned to her work.

Monica went straight to the filing cabinet and yanked open the drawer. She took one last look at the doll's pretty painted china face and pale blue eyes before putting it inside. *Good-bye, doll,* she thought. *I hope Allegra will find you here.*

She placed the doll in the back of the drawer, lying on its back so that its eyelids closed. Then she shut the drawer, took a deep breath, and glanced at her watch again. It was seven o'clock—exactly.

Just as she reached the door to leave the stacks, she heard a hollow click followed by high-pitched laughter. The click was the sound of a key turning in a lock. The laughter was Bridget's.

Monica tried the doorknob, but it wouldn't turn. It wouldn't budge. Bridget had locked her in.

CHAPTER 15

"**N**O!" Monica said aloud. She tried the knob again, but still it wouldn't move.

"Bridget!" she called. "Bridget, let me out of here!"

There was no answer, but Monica knew Bridget was standing silently on the other side of the door.

"Please let me out!" she said. "I'm going to be late for dinner!"

Again there was no answer. Now Monica could hear footsteps receding across the wooden floor.

Suddenly all the lights in the stacks went out, leaving Monica in the dark. She started banging on the door, but it was no use, because she heard the slamming of the main library door then.

She was trapped. Trapped in the dark.

Panic began to rise inside her. *Stay calm, stay calm,* she said to herself. She remembered reading that deep breathing led to relaxation. She took two deep, slow breaths and thought about her situation.

She was locked in a strange room in the dark. That was all right, though. She had been in the dark many times in her life, and it had never hurt her.

But there were worse things to consider. If she didn't get out soon, she'd miss dinner. Skipping a meal without an excuse was considered a serious infraction of the rules at the Chilleen Academy. Since she was already on probation, it might be enough to get her expelled. Bridget probably knew that.

At the thought of Bridget and the trouble she had put Monica through, Monica's fear turned to anger. She couldn't let Bridget get away with this. No way! *I have to find a way out of here,* she thought. As far as she knew, there was only one door. Maybe there was another door somewhere among the bookshelves—an emergency exit.

She began to feel her way along the walls of the room, hoping to find a door she hadn't noticed before. But she circled the room and got all the way back to where she had started without finding anything.

Then she had another thought. Maybe there was an extra key to the room—one for people to use if they accidentally got locked in. *There must be another key,* she thought. *But where would it be?*

It seemed that the most logical place to hang a key would be on the end of one of the tall bookshelves. Monica began to walk among the bookcases, her fingers carefully searching the ends of the tall cases for hooks that might have a key. Her eyes were now beginning to adjust to the dark. Carefully, she went from one end of each bookcase to the next. The scent of old, dusty books filled her nostrils. As she turned a corner and began to search a new bookcase, she heard a sound—a rustling. It was coming from the opposite side of the room.

For a moment she held her breath and stopped moving, straining her ears to hear more. Silence.

A book must have fallen, she thought. Maybe I jostled a book while I was checking the shelves. Then, more quickly, she resumed her search for a key.

Rustle.

There it was again—the same noise. This time it seemed to come from the same side of the room she was on.

Another book, she thought.

Rustle, rustle.

The sound was very faint—it sounded like dry leaves blowing in the wind—but it was real, and it was moving closer. She couldn't ignore it any longer. Someone was in there with her. Someone or something.

Monica's panic returned. She gave up her search for a key and began to run through the stacks away from the sound.

Now she was at the back of the long room. The musty smell was so strong, it made her cough.

There had to be a way out, some way to escape.

Rustle.

Rustle, rustle.

Monica turned a corner and felt something brush her face, something soft and sticky. Stifling a scream, she reached up to pull it away. It was a cobweb. Only a cobweb.

Rustle.

The sound was right behind her now. She spun around, her heart pounding fiercely in her chest.

There was a faint light moving from behind the bookcase directly in front of her. It moved around the bookcase and was now near enough for her to touch. Monica didn't reach out, though. She only stared—fascinated and terrified—at the shimmering figure of the ghost of Allegra Chilleen.

CHAPTER 16

FOR a long moment Monica stared silently at the ghost.

Allegra, with her solemn face and strange heart-shaped birthmark, stared back.

"What—what do you want?" Monica finally asked, her voice little more than a whisper.

In answer Allegra slowly reached a hand out to Monica. Then she began to move toward her.

"No!" Monica shouted, turning and running away. Her heart was beating so hard, it felt as if it would burst. She ran back through the stacks toward the front of the room, her whole body trembling. Monica glanced back over her shoulder and gasped. The ghost-girl was right behind her, having effortlessly and gracefully followed along.

Again, Allegra, wearing an imploring expression on her face, reached out her hand toward Monica.

She wants me, Monica thought. *But for what? To kill me?* She took off for the back of the room and tripped on a small wooden stool, falling against one of the shelves. Several books fell to the floor as she pulled herself upright. When she dared to look back again, she saw the ghost right behind her—calm as ever.

Raising her eyes to the ceiling, she saw a faint silhouette, of ironwork. She remembered the catwalk that ran along the top of the room.

Monica climbed the ancient iron stairs hoping the structure was strong enough to hold her. Each step groaned under her weight. Looking down, she saw that the ghost hadn't moved and was standing at the bottom, gazing up at her.

Maybe, for some reason, the ghost couldn't come up there. Monica continued to climb, trying not to think about how high she was. She couldn't be that much higher than the highest bar in the uneven parallel bars.

At last she reached the top of the catwalk and gingerly stepped onto the open grillwork. At one end of it she could see a faint yellowish glow.

Her heart leaped in sudden excitement and hope. Monica realized that the glow was a window that had been painted over!

Balancing herself the way she did for the balance beam, she ran lightly along the catwalk toward the window. It was a small dormer window, not much larger than two feet square. But it would be big enough for Monica to squeeze through.

The window was secured with an old-fashioned handle and latch. Monica began twisting and turning on the old handle, and at last she felt it give. With all her strength she pushed on the window, and finally it opened about a foot. But would it be wide enough for her to squeeze through? She sat back, catching her breath for a moment. At a sudden noise, she turned and saw that Allegra was on the catwalk, her arms outstretched, moving toward her.

Without even thinking, Monica lunged toward the window and squeezed through.

The next thing she knew, she was standing in the moonlight on the rough shingles of a sloping roof. Far below her the sidewalk of the academy looked impossibly tiny. She had never realized that the building was so high!

The roof that covered most of the main building seemed to be a mile below her, but she knew it really wasn't farther than a story.

She looked back at the dormer window of the library and saw Allegra Chilleen's face shining out at her. *I want you*, the ghost seemed to be saying.

You're not going to get me! Monica thought.

She sat down and carefully scooted toward the edge of the steep roof. Directly below her now was the roof that covered the main floor of the academy. It was a long drop, but she had no choice.

Remembering her gymnastics training, Monica looked at the roof, gauged the distance, and focused all her attention on the landing she would make.

She took a deep breath, moved forward, and dropped—she made a perfect landing in the center of the roof. She could no longer see the little dormer window and had no way of knowing if Allegra was still staring out at her.

Again she scooted over to the edge of the roof. Directly

below, not more than five feet down, was the roof to the front porch.

This part would be easy—almost like a dismount from the uneven parallel bars. She was focusing her attention as before when she was interrupted by a familiar, surprised voice:

"Hey—what are you doing up there?"

CHAPTER 17

MONICA froze.

"Hey, Monica—what are you doing up there?" the voice repeated.

Monica relaxed when she recognized Jimmy's voice. "I'm looking for a cat," she said. It was the first thing that came to her mind.

"You're what?" Jimmy stared at her in obvious disbelief.

"You know that orange cat that belongs to the cook?" Monica said quickly. "Well, I saw her limping earlier, and then I thought I saw her come up here—"

"Right," said Jimmy, laughing. "Well, come on down. Let's go eat. If we hurry, they may still be serving."

Monica moved to where the porch roof sloped toward a trellis and lightly dropped to the ground. She then followed Jimmy into the main building and through the hall to the bustling dining room. Delicious smells filled the air.

After everything that had happened that day, Monica was suddenly ravenous. She ordered mashed potatoes, biscuits, creamed chicken, spinach, a salad, and two cupcakes.

"Are you going to eat all of that?" Jimmy asked, surprised.

"Just watch," said Monica.

As they made their way to an empty table, Monica saw Bridget eating with her friends. Bridget raised her head, and when she saw Monica her eyes opened wide in surprise. But a moment later she turned back to her friends.

Surprised, Bridget? Monica thought. *Well, I've got a lot more surprises up my sleeve.*

Monica ate her food hungrily, laughing and talking with Jimmy and a friend of his who joined them, whose name was Jeff. She was in a better mood than she'd been in since coming to Chilleen Academy—even better than when she'd won the gymnastics meet. *It's so good to be here*, she thought, *with good friends and good food*. The warm feeling stayed with her as she climbed the stairs to her room. *Bridget thought she could stop me, but she couldn't. And Allegra . . .*

At the thought of Allegra, Monica shivered. But relief flooded through her again when she opened the door to her room. With the doll gone, the room no longer felt haunted. Instead, it was just her room—Monica's room.

I'm through with Allegra, she thought. *I've given her what she wanted. The doll is back with the Chilleen family things, where it belongs.*

She got ready for bed and crawled beneath the covers and fell into the deepest and most peaceful sleep she'd had in weeks.

"That color looks great on you," Monica said to Kim, finally seeing her friend in the sweater she had lent her a few days earlier. "It also looks perfect with your bracelet."

"Thanks for letting me wear it," Kim said. "It's so soft, I might never give it back." She laughed.

"Keep it as long as you want. I got it from my aunt for my last birthday, but it's a little small on me."

"Really? You can wear anything of mine whenever you want. I wish my aunt got me sweaters instead of books for my birthday."

"At least you got that bracelet," said Monica. "I wish someone would get me a bracelet like yours."

As they walked to their first period English class, Monica told Kim what had happened in the library.

"When I saw all that Chilleen stuff," she finished, "I realized that the doll should be there too."

"But then why did Allegra show up again?"

"I think she probably stays in the library most of the time," said Monica. "Near her family's things. When I saw her I just panicked. I was sure she was after me. Now I think she was just chasing me out of the library so she could be alone with her doll."

"I don't know," said Kim. "The whole thing is too strange."

"Everything about the Chilleens is strange."

"What about your paper?" said Kim. "Are you still going to write about the Chilleens?"

"I can't." Monica told Kim about Bridget stealing her topic.

"That's so unfair!" said Kim. "Mr. Taylor should have let you do yours on the Chilleens too."

"I know. I was really mad for a while, but I found out what I needed to. It doesn't really matter anymore. Besides, the main thing is that Allegra has her doll back, and she's not going to bother me anymore."

"I hope you're right," said Kim.

"I know I am. I just feel it. I still have to pick a new topic, though. Come on, I'll race you to class."

Laughing, the girls ran around the back of the main building to the classroom annex.

Monica was a few steps behind her friend when Kim suddenly skidded to a stop. "What's the matter?" Monica asked. "Giving up already?"

And then she stopped too.

Pulling away from the front of the building was an orange and white ambulance. A small crowd stood in the driveway, staring after the vehicle.

"What happened?" Kim asked a redheaded boy next to her.

"It's Mr. Taylor," he replied. "The history teacher. He had a heart attack."

CHAPTER 18

"**M**R. Taylor?" Monica couldn't believe her ears.

"Yeah," the boy said. "One minute the dude was standing up, talking to the kids going into his class, and the next minute he keeled over."

"You mean he's *dead?*" Monica asked, horrified.

"I don't know," said the boy. "But I can tell you he didn't look good lying there."

All My Wishes, Monica thought. *I was so angry at Mr. Taylor, I wished I could have a different history teacher. And now I will.*

"Monica, are you all right?" Kim sounded worried. "You're so pale."

"I was just thinking about Mr. Taylor," Monica said.

"I'm sure he'll be all right," said Kim reassuringly. "My uncle had a heart attack last summer, and in six weeks he was—"

"You don't understand!" Monica interrupted. "Kim, I think I *caused* it!"

"You *what?*"

"Kim, remember the necklace the doll was wearing— the one that said 'All Your Wishes'?" Kim nodded, confused. "I think it has the power to *make* wishes come true."

"What do you mean?" said Kim. "What wishes?"

"Well, for instance, I wished I'd beat Bridget in the gymnastics meet. Then she had that accident. Then I wished I had a leather jacket, and Bridget's jacket showed up in my closet." As she listened to herself explain things to Kim, Monica realized that what she was saying sounded crazy. But she also knew she was right.

"Whoa," said Kim. "Are you saying you wished Mr. Taylor would have a heart attack?"

"Of course not," said Monica. "But I was so angry with him about the paper that I wished I could be in Mrs. Douglas's class."

"All those things are probably just coincidences," said Kim after a moment.

"Maybe. But I don't think so. I think this just proves how evil Allegra is."

"I don't know, Mon. I think you're imagining things, but I'm glad you got rid of the doll."

"Me too."

"Don't worry about it anymore, okay?"

"Okay," said Monica. But in her mind she saw again the ambulance as it drove away with Mr. Taylor.

Monica yawned. Her clock showed it was after midnight, which meant she'd been working on her English essay for over four hours. Her eyes were tired from working by the dim light of the small desk lamp. The "lights out" rule had gone into effect an hour ago, and she couldn't afford to get into any more trouble. But she was so behind in her homework, she just had to keep at it.

She stretched luxuriously, arching her back and reaching her hands high into the air, before reaching for her algebra book. *I'll do a page of math problems before calling it a night,* she told herself.

She took out a fresh sheet of paper and began working on the first problem.

"If a plane leaves Chicago at twelve noon Central Time," she read aloud, "and a plane takes off from Denver at 3:00 P.M. Mountain Time—"

Thump.

Startled, Monica looked up from her book. It sounded as if there were something out on the stairs.

Thump.

There it was again—faint but clear. *Maybe it's just the building settling,* she told herself. But just to be safe, she got up and slipped a chair under the doorknob. Then she had to laugh at herself when she realized she was trying to keep out a ghost that could move *through* chairs and doors. And anyway, there was no ghost anymore, she reminded herself. The whole thing seemed so crazy.

Turning back to her math book, she tried to focus on the problem again. *The plane leaving Chicago left at noon,* she reminded herself. She read it again. "And a plane takes off from Denver at 3:00 P.M. Mountain Time . . ."

Monica read the problem over and over, trying to understand what she was supposed to do. She'd never been great at word problems, and besides, she was too exhausted to think straight. Then it dawned on her that what she was really doing was waiting for Alle—

Thump.

Thump, thump.

There was no doubt about it. Someone was coming up the stairs.

Holding her breath, Monica strained to hear more. Who could it be? And why was the person climbing so slowly?

Thump . . . thump.

Monica felt a shiver pass down her back. She shut her math book—the plane problem would have to wait.

Maybe it's one of my friends, she thought. *Maybe it's Jimmy. Maybe he can't sleep and wants to talk.*

Thump.

But why would he climb the stairs so strangely? It sounded like a thing—not a person.

Thump!

The last thump was loudest, and seemed to be right outside Monica's bedroom door. She strained her ears, waiting to hear more. All she heard was silence.

Someone must be playing a joke on me, she thought angrily, picturing Bridget's face in her mind. *Well, whoever it is, is going to be sorry!*

She stood up, tiptoed across the room, removed the chair from under the doorknob, and yanked the door open. There was no one there. The hallway was dark and empty. But then she looked straight down at her feet and stifled a scream.

Sitting propped against the doorjamb, its eyes glowing red, was Allegra Chilleen's doll.

"No," Monica whispered. "Please, no."

But the doll continued to sit there, staring straight into Monica's eyes.

How did it get here? she wondered.

Allegra brought it back was the answer, the only answer. *She's still after me*, Monica thought in despair. *How can I get rid of a ghost if I can't even get rid of a doll?*

CHAPTER 19

"KIM! You'll never believe what happened!" Monica was so relieved to see her friend the next morning that she didn't notice Kim's red and puffy eyes. She had already begun telling Kim about the doll when she noticed that something was wrong.

"What's wrong, Kimmie?" Monica said. "Please—stop crying."

"I can't help it." Kim sniffed. "I've looked everywhere, but it's gone!" It was just after breakfast, and Kim had stopped by Monica's room before class. She was crying hysterically now and trying to tell Monica that her new bracelet had disappeared.

"It's got to be somewhere," Monica said, knotting a piece of red yarn around the end of her thick braid. "We can put a lost-and-found note on the bulletin board."

"Monica!" Kim shouted, forgetting about the bracelet. Monica turned and saw Kim pointing toward the bureau.

"What's that doll doing back here?" Kim asked. For

the first time since she'd come in, Kim studied Monica closely. "You look terrible. Are you feeling okay?"

"That's what I wanted to tell you," said Monica. "She's after me. Allegra's trying to get me."

"She *had* her doll back," said Kim, wiping her eyes on her sleeve. "What more did she want?"

"I have no idea." Monica went on to tell Kim about the doll showing up at her door the night before. "So I don't know what to do with the doll. Every time I take it off the bureau, it comes back. At least if I leave it there, I won't have to wonder how it got there. It'll be there because *I* put it there."

"Maybe Bridget brought it up here," said Kim. "Remember, she saw you in the stacks with the doll."

"But why would she do that, Kimmie? She doesn't know the doll belongs to Allegra Chilleen. Besides, she thinks dolls are stupid."

"But she also has a grudge against you. Plus she has a key to the stacks."

"I'd love for you to be right," said Monica, "but I'm sure it was Allegra. Kimmie, what am I going to do?"

"You can move in with my family."

"No, really," said Monica. "I seriously don't know what to do."

"Wait a minute, Mon. If the doll's necklace can make your wishes come true, why can't you wish the doll away or wish that Allegra would leave you alone?"

"I don't think it works that way," said Monica.

"Well, you have to get rid of the doll." Kim's voice sounded calm, but Monica could see that her friend was almost as upset as she was. "If you keep it in here," Kim went on, "Allegra will just keep coming back."

"But she won't let me get rid of it," Monica wailed. "When I put it back in the closet it came back, and in the library—"

"Maybe you just didn't take it far enough away," said Kim suddenly.

"Huh?"

"Well, you keep taking it to places at school. Maybe you should take it into town or something."

"You just gave me an idea," Monica said, suddenly calmer. "It's kind of scary, but it just might work. In fact, it might be the only thing that will work."

"What is it?"

"Well, you'll have to be willing to break a school rule," said Monica. "Are you?"

"Come on, Monica." Kim sounded impatient. "What do I have to do?"

"Stay in my room tonight. I know it's not allowed without Mrs. Danita's permission, but no one has to know. You can come up here after gymnastics, and I'll sneak you some food from dinner. I have two extra blankets that I can fold up and put on the floor."

"I'll do that," said Kim. "I'll tell my parents you have permission for me to stay so they won't worry. Then I can help you in case Allegra shows up again."

"*That's* not why I want you to stay," said Monica. "I want you to help me make sure she never *does* show up again."

"Now I'm totally confused. What are you talking about?"

"About what you just said," said Monica. "About not taking the doll far enough away. Well, I just realized where it has to go. I should have thought of it before."

"Where?" said Kim.

"Where Allegra is. I mean, where she *really* is—the Chilleen graveyard."

"Are you crazy?" Kim said quietly. She stared at her friend.

"Think about it, Kim. Allegra's dead and buried. The only way to get her and the doll together is to bury it with her."

"I see what you mean," said Kim after a moment. "But what if someone sees us?"

"That's why I want you to stay over. We'll do it tonight, after everyone's in bed. That is, if you'll help me."

Kim's face turned very pale beneath her freckles. "Sure," she finally said. "Why not?"

Walking as quietly as she could, Monica led the way down the stairs. Kim followed closely behind her. Against her back, Monica could feel the snug weight of the day pack, which contained the doll, a flashlight, and the two soup spoons she had slipped out of the cafeteria after dinner. Both girls wore jeans and sneakers.

The huge grandfather clock in the main hall began to chime midnight, making other things vibrate throughout the ancient house. *Perfect timing*, Monica thought as she slipped the lock open on the front door. The sounds of the clock would block out any sounds they made.

What am I doing? Monica thought as they stepped out into the night. *I'm on probation. If I get caught, I'll be kicked out of school.* But she also knew she had no choice and quietly closed the door.

The chill air was moist and smelled of pine and damp vegetation. Pausing a second, Monica let her eyes adjust to the darkness. A thin crescent moon shone above the trees, and Monica thought once again how beautiful the area was.

"Don't just stand there," whispered Kim. "Let's get it over with."

Monica nodded and started across the broad, grassy lawn, leading her friend into the pine forest. She hoped they wouldn't run into Mr. Fernandez, the school security guard.

"It's so dark out here," whispered Kim.

Monica pulled the flashlight out of her pack and switched it on. The small circle of light somehow made the thick forest less threatening. "Come on," she said. "It's this way."

Shivering from more than the chill, she led Kim through the forest, along the same path the ghost of Allegra had led her.

An owl hooted overhead. Monica jumped without meaning to and immediately began searching for Allegra. But the ghost was nowhere in sight.

Good, Monica thought. *Just stay away from me and I'll give you back your stupid doll.*

"Monica?" Kim's voice sounded tired and scared. Monica turned her attention to her friend.

"What's the matter?" Monica asked.

"Nothing. But is it much farther?"

"I don't think so. I think it's right over—"

But Monica's words were cut off by a piercing shriek from Kim. With her heart pounding, Monica whirled around.

Her friend was gone.

CHAPTER 20

"**K**IM!" Monica screamed out her friend's name. What could have happened to her?

"Help!" Monica heard Kim's voice coming from down low. She swung the flashlight around to shine on a ditch that had been half-hidden by a fallen tree and a carpet of leaves and pinecones.

"Kim!" Monica called. "Are you all right?"

"I think so." Kim's small, round face looked pale and frightened. "Help me out—it's all slimy down here!"

Leaning over, Monica reached down with her hand. The ditch was filled with wet, decaying needles and leaves.

Kim grabbed Monica's hand and with her help, scrambled up the slippery slope. "Yuck," she said, brushing off her jeans. "I'm all wet and muddy!"

"Look at that!" said Monica, pointing to a spot where the path had given way into the ditch.

"No wonder I fell in," said Kim. "I was so scared. At first I thought I fell into a grave."

"Stay close to me," said Monica. "I'll keep the flashlight right on the path."

The girls moved cautiously along the path until they came to the clearing. It was thick with weeds and decaying plants. "This is it," she whispered.

The clearing contained many tombstones, which cast eerie shadows in the dim moonlight. There were stones of every size and shape, most of them weather-beaten and crumbling with age.

Monica bent down to look at a nearby stone. "Baby Jim Chilleen, Nov. 1–Nov. 2, 1897," she read.

"I wonder how many people are buried here?" said Kim in a shaky voice.

"All the Chilleens. Or most of them, anyway." *And I hope they stay buried,* Monica thought.

"How will we ever find Allegra's grave?" Kim went on.

Monica had been wondering the same thing. "We'll just have to search." At the thought of searching a graveyard, a shiver went down her spine.

"That could take all night!" said Kim.

"We'll just have to hurry," said Monica.

Kim nodded, but Monica could see that her friend was really scared—even more scared than she herself was. *Maybe it wasn't fair to ask Kim to come along,* she thought. *After all, it's my problem, not hers.*

"Come on," Kim said impatiently.

Hastily Monica began to sweep the flashlight beam along the nearby stones. She recognized the names of some of the first Chilleens—Ebenezer, Aldrich, and Cuthbert.

"I think this is the old part of the graveyard," she told Kim. "Let's try over there."

The girls began to walk across the family burial ground when they saw a sudden movement just in front of them.

Kim gave a small shriek and grabbed Monica's arm. "What was that?" she cried.

"There it is again!" said Monica. The indistinct shape disappeared behind a tall tombstone.

"It's one of the Chilleens," said Kim, her voice shaking. "They don't want us here!"

"We can't leave, we've got to bury the—"

The shape darted out from behind the stone, rustling some dead leaves.

"Come on, let's get out of here!" said Kim, starting to run back toward the path.

"Kim, wait!" cried Monica. She started after her friend, and at that moment the shape darted straight at her, stopped, turned, and moved back toward the forest. Forcing her arm to stay steady, Monica swung the flashlight toward the shape. Laughing, she swung it down in relief. Bounding out of the clearing and into the forest was the "ghost"—a small gray rabbit.

"It's just a rabbit," she called across the clearing.

"Are you sure?"

"Look," said Monica, raising the flashlight as Kim approached. "There it goes."

"Maybe it's a Chilleen rabbit," said Kim, and then she started to giggle. Monica started giggling too.

"I can't believe this," Kim said, gasping for breath. "Here we are out in a graveyard in the middle of the night, laughing!"

"Come on," said Monica. "Let's find Allegra."

They continued to check out the gravestones. Finally Monica found a familiar name. "Valentine Chilleen," she said. "That's her father! Her grave has to be right near his."

"I see it!" said Kim. Both girls stepped up to a dark stone with weeds growing around it. Carved in simple block letters were the words ALLEGRA CHILLEEN, 1899–1911.

Monica continued to stare at the stone. *So this is where you're buried,* she thought. *Well, you can stay here now because I've brought your doll back.*

She set her pack on the ground, and then, without a word, took out the spoons. "Here, Kim," she said. "Take a spoon." They began to dig right next to the grave of Allegra Chilleen.

"What if we dig up a skeleton?" said Kim after a few minutes.

"Don't even say that!" said Monica. But she had been worrying about the same thing.

A moment later Kim shrieked in terror.

"What is it?" Monica asked, her heart thudding.

"I found a—a . . ." Kim couldn't finish the sentence, but shone the flashlight on a brown, wet, wriggling thing amid the clods of dirt.

Monica moved back involuntarily and then relaxed. "It's just an earthworm!"

"Oh," said Kim, sounding disgusted. "I thought it was—never mind what I thought." She took a deep breath and resumed digging. The ground was damp from recent rains, and it wasn't hard for the girls to make a hole a foot long and nearly as deep—the perfect amount of space for the doll.

Looking at the pile of damp earth beside the hole, Monica wiped her hands on her jeans. Then carefully she took the doll out of her pack and laid it down in the hole.

"Here, Allegra," she whispered. "Here's your doll."

"Hurry," said Kim. "Cover it up."

THE EVIL ONE

Monica took a last look at the doll. Then, with Kim's help, she began to push handfuls of dirt back into the hole. She watched with satisfaction as the dark earth fell on the doll's white china face. The last part covered was the eyelids. When the doll was completely buried, they filled in the rest of the hole.

Monica stood, dusted off her hands, and put her pack back on.

"It's over," she told Kim. "It's all over now."

CHAPTER 21

"**W**AKE up, sleepyhead."

Monica opened her eyes to see Kim sitting at the foot of her bed. Kim had already put away the blankets she had slept on.

Monica stretched and sat up. "What time is it?"

"About fifteen minutes till breakfast," said her friend. "My back is killing me from sleeping on the floor."

"Sorry."

"Oh, well," said Kim. "Just so it doesn't screw up my backflips."

Monica stretched. "I really slept," she said. "I guess it's just knowing we got rid of the you-know-what."

"I still don't believe we did that," said Kim.

"Me neither. Someday when we're old we can tell our grandchildren how we went out to a graveyard in the middle of the night to bury a doll."

"They'll think we were crazy!" Kim laughed.

Monica got up and picked up a navy blue turtleneck from her clean laundry pile.

Kim began to repack her overnight bag, leaving out clean clothes to wear. "Uh-oh," she said.

"What's wrong?"

"I thought I could wear the same jeans I wore yesterday, but they're all torn and muddy," said Kim. "Look."

"Whoa," said Monica. "That must have happened when you fell in the ditch. I didn't even notice last night."

"Me neither. Can I wear a pair of yours?"

"Sure," said Monica. "They're in the bottom drawer."

Monica was just pulling on her own jeans when she heard Kim gasp. "I don't believe it!" Kim cried.

"What?" said Monica, wondering for a heart-stopping moment if the doll had come back.

"Look what I found in your drawer!" said Kim.

Monica turned and saw that her friend's face was twisted in shock and pain. In Kim's hand was the silver Navajo bracelet her parents had given her for her birthday.

"How'd that get in my drawer?" Monica asked, surprised and confused.

"Good question," said Kim, obviously upset.

"Do you think *I* put it there?" said Monica.

"Who else could have put it there?" said Kim, her expression changing from confused to angry. "I'm sorry, but this ghost stuff is getting too weird for me. I don't know what to believe anymore."

"Kimmie! You *know* I'd never take your bracelet!" Monica was stunned. "I have no idea who put it there."

"And you also don't know who put Bridget's leather jacket in your closet," said Kim angrily. "I'm starting to think this whole ghost business is your way of getting *everything* you want without it being your fault."

"How can you say that?" said Monica.

"I don't know what to believe, Monica! All I know is this is the second time something stolen has turned up in your room!"

"Kim, no, listen to me—"

"I'm through listening to you. I've been listening to you all semester!" Kim threw the pair of Monica's jeans she'd been holding on the floor and began to pull on her own torn, muddy ones. "You really had me fooled, you know? I actually believed all that stuff about Allegra Chilleen and the doll. I actually believed that you didn't steal Bridget's jacket. I must be the dumbest person in Phantom Valley!"

"I didn't take the bracelet!" Monica said in despair.

"If you wanted it so much, why didn't you just tell me?" Kim's voice began to shake. "I would have let you wear it any time you wanted!"

"Kim, please—"

"And I thought we were such good friends," Kim went on, gathering up her overnight bag and school books. "But there's no way I can be friends with someone who's a liar and a thief!"

Her face was streaming with tears as she rushed out of the room and slammed the door.

Monica pulled open the door and ran after her, her face hot with humiliation. "Kim, please wait, please, Kim—"

Kim stopped at the top of the stairs and whirled around. "Wait for what?" she asked. "More of your lies? Are you going to tell me that Allegra Chilleen stole my bracelet and put it in your drawer?"

"I don't know how it got there!" said Monica. "But I think Allegra had something to do with it. But, Kim, she's gone now!"

"So am I!" said Kim. "Forget it, Monica, just forget

it!" She turned around again and bent her head forward. Suddenly her shoulders started to shake and she burst into tears.

Monica just stood there. She wanted to comfort her friend, but she didn't know what to say. From downstairs she heard sounds of kids going to breakfast.

Then, suddenly, she felt a pressure at her back—a firm and steady pressure pushing her forward. Pushing her toward Kim, who was still sobbing on the top step of the stairs.

Monica's arms rose in the air, till they were stretched out straight in front of her. The force continued to press her forward. She tried to fight against it but found she was unable to control her arms or the steps she was taking toward Kim. Desperately Monica realized that if she couldn't find a way to stop it, the force would push her directly into Kim. It would make her push Kim down the stairs.

Monica twisted her head around to look behind her. There she saw Allegra Chilleen, madness radiating from her eyes.

CHAPTER 22

MONICA fought against the pressure. What was Allegra doing? Was she trying to make Monica push her best friend down the stairs?

"No!" she shouted, terrified.

At that moment she felt herself lunging forward, but Kim had already started down the stairs. Monica fell against the wall at the top of the staircase.

"It's no use, Monica," Kim said, not even turning around. "I hope that someday you—you get the help you need." Quickly she continued down the stairs.

Monica steadied herself against the wall and then turned back to face the ghost of Allegra Chilleen. But the hall was empty. Allegra was gone.

It was no use telling herself she had just imagined it— this had happened too many times. Only seconds earlier Allegra had been standing behind her, trying to make her hurt Kim. It must have been Allegra who had taken Kim's bracelet and hidden it in her drawer, Monica thought. Now Kim was her enemy—possibly forever. And there wasn't a thing Monica could do about it.

Near tears, she went back to her room.

This can't go on any longer! she thought. *Somehow I've got to stop Allegra.* She shut the door, and as she started to gather up her school books she noticed a muddy streak on the floor, which she hadn't remembered seeing before.

Monica followed the streak. It extended from the bureau, across the room, to her bed—and there, leaning against her pillow, was Allegra's doll! It was covered with dried mud and bits of decayed leaves.

"No," she whispered in horror. "No, no, no!"

The doll stared at Monica, its eyes glowing red. But Monica noticed that something was different. The doll's expression had changed. Instead of the closed mouth and slight smile, the doll's lips were parted, and it seemed to be laughing. Laughing at Monica.

"No!" Monica shouted out loud. There was a slight movement at the corner of her vision, which Monica thought to be Allegra floating toward the door.

Quickly she spun around, but the ghost-girl had again vanished.

"You can't do this to me!" she shouted at empty air. "Do you hear me, Allegra?" She ran toward the door and pulled it open. She was sure the ghost had gone into the hall. "Allegra? Allegra!"

She ran out into the hall, not thinking about anything except finding Allegra and confronting her. She had to make her stop what she was doing. "Allegra!" she shouted, running halfway down the stairs.

"Who's Allegra?" called a voice. Monica realized she'd been shouting. At the foot of the stairs had gathered a half dozen students looking up at her. "What are you shouting about, Monica?" asked Jimmy, puzzled.

"Yeah, Monica, what are you shouting about?" added a sarcastic voice.

Monica saw Bridget standing with the other students, her face twisted in a mocking smile.

"Nothing," Monica said in a panic. "Nothing at all. Nothing!" With that, she turned and fled back up the stairs.

She flung open the door of her room, hoping that Allegra had taken the doll away. No such luck. The doll still lay on her pillow, staining the white linen with dirt from the grave. Its face was still twisted in a hideous smile.

I've got to get out of here, Monica thought. All the trouble started because I moved into Allegra's room. The trouble with the doll, with Bridget, and with Kim. Maybe if I move out, Allegra will leave me alone.

She knew she was late for English class, but she didn't care. All she cared about was getting as far away from Allegra as she could.

She splashed water on her face, combed her hair, and went down the stairs to the headmistress's office. Taking a deep breath, she knocked on Mrs. Danita's door. By the time she heard a quiet "Come in," she had already pushed the door open.

"Well, Monica," said Mrs. Danita, raising her eyebrows in surprise. "Shouldn't you be in your first-period class?"

"I didn't go," Monica admitted. "Mrs. Danita, I—I have to talk to you—please."

"Of course, dear," said Mrs. Danita. "Have a seat." She gestured to a chair in front of her desk.

Monica sat down, trying to think of something to say. How could she convince Mrs. Danita to help her? She couldn't tell her the truth—that she was being haunted by the ghost of a girl who had been dead for almost a hundred years.

"Go on, Monica," said Mrs. Danita. "What's troubling you?"

"It's my room," Monica blurted out. "Mrs. Danita, please, please transfer me to a different room."

"Why on earth would you want a new room?" Mrs. Danita said. "You're one of the few students who's lucky enough to have a room of her own."

"I know," said Monica. "But it's— I'm too lonely up there. I think you were right that I need more time to get used to living at school."

The headmistress pursed her lips, appearing quite concerned. "I'm sorry, Monica," she said. "Even if I thought it was a good idea to move you, I couldn't. There are simply no empty rooms."

"Then maybe I could trade with someone," Monica said desperately. "Someone with a roommate who'd like a room of her own."

Mrs. Danita shook her head. "No one has come to me requesting a private room," she said. "And it is rather late in the semester."

"Please," Monica said again. "I really think I need a roommate."

Mrs. Danita studied her for a long moment. "Monica, you're not in a very good position to be asking for favors. You are on probation, remember."

"I know," Monica said miserably. Suddenly she wondered if Kim had told Mrs. Danita about the bracelet. She must not have. If she had, Mrs. Danita would have said something by now. What else could go wrong? she wondered.

"You seem extremely upset," Mrs. Danita said. "Don't you like it here in Phantom Valley?"

"That's the trouble," said Monica. "I love it here. I feel as if I belong here." She remembered how happy she'd been at the beginning of the semester—then she thought about how awful everything was now.

"Perhaps it's just that you're away from home," Mrs. Danita went on. "Not all girls your age are ready for a boarding school experience."

"That's not it," protested Monica. "Really. It's just—just the room. I don't want to be in that room."

"Well, I'm sorry. I can't do anything about the room. Perhaps I should call your parents in Italy."

"Please don't do that." Monica thought of her parents and how upset and worried they'd be if they heard from Mrs. Danita—especially if they had to come take her away from Chilleen Academy.

"I don't know what else to do," said Mrs. Danita.

"Please don't do anything. Never mind. I'll—I'll just have to get used to the room somehow. I'm sorry I bothered you."

She left the headmistress's office in despair. No one was going to help her, she realized. Not Mrs. Danita, not Kim, not anyone. It was going to be up to her alone to figure out what to do about Allegra Chilleen.

Never before in her life had Monica felt so alone.

CHAPTER 23

MONICA passed the rest of the day as if in a dream. She went to her classes and answered when the other kids spoke to her, but she felt as if she were in a different world.

I'm alone, she kept thinking. *All alone—except for Allegra.*

She felt so terrible, she couldn't eat her dinner. She just stared at her plate of fried chicken and rice as if they were cardboard. Once she glanced over at Bridget's table, expecting to see Bridget's mocking smile, but Bridget was absorbed laughing and talking with her friends.

Wondering if she'd ever be able to joke around again, Monica took her tray to the kitchen area. Ignoring several friends' greetings, she left the cafeteria and trudged up to her room—Allegra's room.

She picked up the muddy doll from her bed and put it back on the bureau. She remembered how happy she had been her first few days in Phantom Valley. She had felt so at home. She remembered her first sight of the room, how cheery and cozy it had seemed.

But the room no longer seemed friendly. Instead it seemed dangerous, with evil lurking in every shadow.

It's getting hard to breathe in here! she thought, going to the window and pulling it open. It was raining, and a cool breeze blew into the room. She could just make out the tall shapes of the pine trees beyond the lawn. But now even the forest seemed possessed of evil, of danger.

Her eyes filled with tears as she returned to her bed, and sat propped up against the wall as the doll had been. From the top of the bureau the doll seemed to be staring malevolently at her. But its face was wearing its usual painted expression. She thought she must have imagined that the face had changed earlier. Monica knew that somehow the doll was the key to her troubles.

Somehow, she thought, *I've got to get the doll back to Allegra. But how?* She felt torn. Allegra scared her, but she had to get through to her so she could take her doll back.

Monica tried to figure out the best way to get to Allegra since Allegra seemed to come and go as she pleased. Maybe if she waited long enough, Allegra would show up. But she didn't want to wait. She wanted to get it over with *now*.

She continued to stare at the doll. She noticed the necklace: "All Your Wishes."

Of course! She could try to use the doll to make Allegra come. She had rejected the idea before, but now she decided it was her last hope.

Without thinking about how dangerous it might be, Monica took the doll off the bureau and held it tight in her arms.

I wish, she thought, shutting her eyes and concentrating, *I wish Allegra would come here to me, now. I wish for Allegra, I wish . . .*

For a moment nothing happened, and then suddenly there was a tremendous flash of lightning, followed by rolling thunder. The lights flickered and then went out. Monica's heart pounded as she opened her eyes. An odd glowing light appeared by the door to the closet, and as Monica watched, it materialized into the form of Allegra Chilleen.

She was as beautiful as she had been the other times she appeared, except that this time she had a strange half smile and was carrying a glowing kerosene lamp. Allegra lifted the lantern higher as if offering it to Monica.

Horrified, Monica remembered the newspaper story she had read about Allegra. How she might have deliberately burned down her family's house with kerosene.

Allegra took a step closer, gesturing for Monica to take the lamp. The fire inside it glowed brighter and brighter.

Oh, no, Monica realized. *She wants to do it again! She wants me to help her burn down the school just the way she killed her own family! She really is evil!*

I can't let her get away with this.

Allegra took another step closer, and now Monica could feel the heat from the flame. The fire in the lamp was real—real enough to burn down the school, to kill dozens of innocent people.

"No," Monica whispered, moving back toward her bed.

Allegra moved closer and opened her mouth. For the first time Monica could hear her ghostly voice as if it were coming from inside her own head.

"Come, Monica," Allegra whispered. "Come. Now we will do it. Now is the time."

"The time for what?" said Monica.

"You know," said Allegra. "You know what must be done."

"No!" Monica cried out loud. At that moment there was a flash of lightning, and the room filled with brilliant light until the rumble of thunder carried it away. Then it became dark again—dark except for the hypnotic glow of the lamp.

"You must," she told Monica, practically forcing her to take the lamp. "I can't do this alone. I need your help."

No, Monica thought. *No, I won't do it. I won't burn down the school. No matter what happens to me, I won't do it!*

"Come," Allegra whispered again. She was right in front of Monica now, and the lantern's heat felt like that from the flames of a roaring fire. "Do it," Allegra whispered. "Help me do it."

Monica felt a ghostly hand guide hers. Unable to resist, Monica felt her hands lift up and remove the glass chimney. Now the flame was open, open to the air.

For a moment Monica and the ghost stood and stared at each other. Allegra's face was intense, as if the only thing in the world that mattered was what they were going to do next.

I won't do it, Monica thought again, but even while she thought this, she felt her hands move again. *No, please no*, she thought, but her hands continued to move against her will.

How will it happen? she wondered.

In horror, she continued to struggle but watched as her trembling hands moved closer to the lamp, reaching for the deadly fire. She had no control over her own hands.

Despairing, she peered into Allegra's eyes. Instead of the madness she expected to see, she saw sorrow.

And then, suddenly, she felt her hands move away from the lantern and down to where the doll lay on the bed. With more strength than she had ever possessed, her hands closed around the doll and brought it up to the open flame.

The room suddenly filled with an eerie, high-pitched howl. Monica continued to hold the doll to the flame even when she felt it begin to move in her hands, squirming and twisting like a snake. But she held it.

The doll's hair began to singe, and then burn. Its once pretty china face began to blacken.

Outside, lightning flashed again, and the room shook with thunder.

The whole doll was on fire now—its dress and head aflame. Yet the odd thing was that though Monica was holding the doll, her hands remained cool and unburned. Suddenly, feeling calmer than she had in a long time, Monica took the doll and threw it outside. She watched as it fell like a brightly burning falling star to the lawn below.

The eerie howling still filled the air, but it was growing weaker and weaker.

Fascinated and horrified, Monica watched as what was left of the doll burned below her until there was nothing left but ashes. Monica felt her whole body relax as a great feeling of peace passed over her.

She looked around the room, which was completely silent, and saw that Allegra was gone. A soft breeze brushed her face, like a loving caress. Very faintly, but distinctly, she heard again the voice of Allegra Chilleen:

Thank you, Monica. You have released us both. Now I can rest at last.

Monica shivered. "Good-bye, Allegra," she whispered, smiling.

Outside the thunderstorm had passed. Monica went to the window and inhaled the fresh scent of wet pine forest.

She leaned outside, straining to see where she had thrown the doll. All that remained was a faint dark patch on the lawn.

EPILOGUE

"I T really is the most beautiful bracelet I've ever seen," Monica told Kim, admiring the silver circle around her friend's wrist.

"I know," Kim said simply.

"The only thing is, I don't *wish* I had it myself," Monica went on. The girls were sitting at a study table in the library. Their books lay forgotten on the table while Monica told Kim everything that had happened the night before.

"Excuse me," said a familiar voice. Both girls raised their heads to see Bridget standing above them. "The library is for studying, not talking," she said, disapproval on her face.

"Sorry," said Monica, not even annoyed.

"We'll be quiet," said Kim.

"I hope so," said Bridget. "Otherwise, you'll have to leave."

"By the way," said Monica, unable to resist, "I've been meaning to ask you. How is your paper on the Chilleens coming along?"

"Oh, that?" said Bridget. "I gave up that topic—it was so boring. Nothing interesting ever happened to that family."

Monica and Kim waited for Bridget to walk away before laughing. After a moment Kim leaned over and began whispering. "I'm sorry I accused you of being a thief, Monica," she said.

"It's okay," said Monica. "That's what the doll wanted you to think."

"Do you think that thing about 'All Your Wishes' was really true?" Kim went on.

"Uh-huh."

"But I thought Allegra was always around when the bad things happened."

"She was," Monica agreed. "But it was because she was trying to protect me. She was doing everything she could to save me from the doll."

Kim shuddered. "So the *doll* was really The Evil One."

"Yes, Kimmie. But for all these years poor Allegra got blamed for the evil. Even you and I thought she was causing everything bad around here."

"Poor Allegra," said Kim.

"I know. Just before she left, I got a feeling about what her life had been like. Before Edward gave her the doll, she was a normal, happy twelve-year-old. But then the doll's evil took over and terrible things started happening. The worst thing was the fire that destroyed her whole family."

"Do you think Edward knew the doll was evil and gave it to her to get back at the Chilleens for letting him go?" said Kim.

"It's possible, but maybe the doll controlled him, too. We'll never know."

"But why was Allegra haunting *you?*" Kim said.

"She wasn't haunting me, specifically. It's just that I was in her room and found her doll. Ever since the fire, she'd been forced to haunt the world, unable to find peace until the doll was destroyed."

"And now she can rest in peace," said Kim.

"Yes," said Monica. "Early this morning, after the doll burned, I got dressed and went out to the cemetery. I picked wildflowers in the woods and put them on Allegra's grave. I could feel she was at peace."

"So it's all over."

"All but one thing." Monica pointed to Bridget, who was shelving books across the room.

Kim looked puzzled. "Bridget didn't have anything to do with Allegra."

"I know," said Monica. "And I want to keep it that way. This is none of her business."

She lifted her pack from the back of her chair, leaned over, and whispered something to Kim. Smiling, Kim nodded, got up from the table, and went over to Bridget.

"Excuse me, Bridget," Monica heard Kim say. "I need three books from the top shelves. Can you help me, please?"

Monica watched as Bridget got the rolling ladder and climbed to the top, reaching for the books Kim had requested. Monica reached into her pack and took out the little framed portrait of Allegra Chilleen. She had spent time that morning cleaning and polishing the old frame.

With another quick glance at Bridget, Monica took the portrait over to the far wall of the library where Allegra's family portraits were hung and carefully placed it on the bare hook at the end of the row.

You're home at last, Allegra, Monica thought. *Home where you belong.*

About the Author

LYNN BEACH was born in El Paso, Texas, and grew up in Tucson, Arizona. She is the author of many fiction and non-fiction books for adults and children.

About the Author

Phantom Valley™

THE DARK

Jason McCormick, who is blind, comes to Chilleen Academy determined to prove to his parents that he can be independent. But he's not there a week before his trusty seeing-eye dog, Erroll, begins to behave very strangely. Erroll bites Jason's roommate and is suspected of hurting Jason himself—he seems to be a completely different dog. And Jason thinks he knows why—Erroll has been possessed by an evil spirit! Jason must fight the evil spirit himself, blind and alone, to save his dog's life—and his own.